‖‖‖ W9-ALL-884

BEWARE!!
DO NOT READ THIS
BOOK FROM
BEGINNING TO END!

Excellent! You've got an automatic A on your science project — because your friend's uncle Darius is going to help you. And Darius is an inventor!

But then Darius tests out his new invention, an elevator that takes people to other dimensions. And when he returns, he's . . . different. You notice this when he tries to cut off your head with a machete.

Oh, no! He's not the real Uncle Darius! He's a copy from a parallel universe. Can you use the elevator to rescue the real Darius? Hurry — before the copy cuts off your head and adds it to his shrunken head collection!

This scary adventure is about you. You decide what will happen — and how terrifying the scares will be!

Start on page 1. Then follow the instructions at the bottom of each page. You make the choices. If you choose well, you'll keep your head. But if you make the wrong choice . . . BEWARE!

SO TAKE A DEEP BREATH. CROSS YOUR FINGERS. AND TURN TO PAGE 1 NOW TO *GIVE YOURSELF GOOSEBUMPS!*

READER BEWARE —
YOU CHOOSE THE SCARE!

Look for more
GIVE YOURSELF GOOSEBUMPS adventures
from R.L. STINE:

R.L. STINE

GIVE YOURSELF

Goosebumps®

ELEVATOR TO NOWHERE

AN
APPLE
PAPERBACK

EAU CLAIRE DISTRICT LIBRARY

SCHOLASTIC INC.
New York Toronto London Auckland Sydney
Mexico City New Delhi Hong Kong

T 115945

A PARACHUTE PRESS BOOK

If you purchased this book without a cover, you should be aware that this book is stolen property. It was reported as "unsold and destroyed" to the publisher, and neither the author nor the publisher has received any payment for this "stripped book."

No part of this publication may be reproduced in whole or in part, or stored in a retrieval system, or transmitted in any form or by any means, electronic, mechanical, photocopying, recording, or otherwise, without written permission of the publisher. For information regarding permission, write to Scholastic Inc., Attention: Permissions Department, 555 Broadway, New York, NY 10012.

ISBN 0-590-51670-1

Copyright © 1999 by Parachute Press, Inc. All rights reserved. Published by Scholastic Inc. APPLE PAPERBACKS and associated logos are trademarks and/or registered trademarks of Scholastic Inc. GOOSEBUMPS is a registered trademark of Parachute Press, Inc.

12 11 10 9 8 7 6 5 4 3 2 1   9/9 0 1 2 3 4/0

Printed in the U.S.A.   40

First Scholastic printing, March 1999

This science project is going to be a snap! You were totally dreading it. Then you got teamed up with Jamie. Not only is she the smartest girl in class — her uncle Darius is a real live inventor!

"With your uncle's help, we'll ace this project," you tell Jamie as you walk toward Darius's house.

"Well, probably," Jamie answers. "The important thing is not to let Uncle Darius get carried away. He can be a little extreme sometimes."

"Extreme?" you repeat.

"Extremely extreme," she warns. "Once he had me test these Escalator Shoes he invented. I was stuck on the ceiling for two hours!"

You picture Jamie hanging upside down and laugh out loud. She punches you in the shoulder.

"Ow!" you cry. She's as strong as she is smart.

"Just don't ask him to demonstrate any of his inventions," she cautions. "They hardly ever work the way you think."

She comes to a stop. "Well, here we are."

When you see the house, your eyes open wide. Really wide.

Go to PAGE 2.

"It's . . . interesting," you manage.

What you mean is — it's creepy! The windows are broken and barred. The paint is flaking off. The yard is full of dead leaves. It looks as if no one has lived there for a hundred years.

"He doesn't keep it up very well," Jamie explains.

"Too busy inventing things, maybe," you suggest.

You jump as something runs across your feet. But then you realize it's just a cat.

"Oh, poor Sapphire." Jamie sighs. "Uncle Darius never remembers to feed her. We'll feed you on the way out, Sapph."

The cat stares hungrily up at you. Then she disappears into the untrimmed bushes.

Jamie pushes open the door. You're surprised the house is so dark. There's not much furniture, just bizarre machines. They seem to crouch in the shadows. Waiting . . .

"He must be in the lab," Jamie whispers.

"Why are we whispering?" you whisper back.

"I don't want to disturb him," she answers. "He's kind of excitable when he's working."

"Extreme and excitable," you mutter. "Great."

Just then a pair of hands grabs your shoulders.

Grab hold of PAGE 3.

The hands lift you up and turn you around.

You find yourself facing an old man wearing a loud Hawaiian shirt and thick glasses. "Hello, Jamie!" he booms.

"I'm over here!" Jamie shouts from behind you.

Uncle Darius squints at you, peers at Jamie, then drops you back to the floor. "That's right, you are!" he declares. "Well, come on into the lab."

You rub your shoulders as you follow the two of them. Darius is *really* strong. Like a giant version of Jamie.

You follow them into the lab. Awesome! Every square inch is filled with gizmos and gadgets.

"You said on the phone that you're doing a science project," Darius says. "I'd be glad to help. I was just about to test my Transuniversal Transvator." He gestures toward a huge machine towering against a wall. It has sliding doors right in the middle, with a big button to one side.

"It looks like an elevator," you observe. Wait a second. This is a one-story house. Why would he build an elevator?

"Yes, but instead of other floors," Darius explains, "it goes to other universes!"

You stare at Darius. Gee, you think. Jamie never mentioned that her uncle was *completely* crazy!

Go to PAGE 4.

4

You decide to humor him. "That sounds cool. Maybe I could take a ride in it."

Right before they cart this guy to the loony bin! you add to yourself.

Jamie punches you again. Ow!

"Too dangerous. Much too dangerous," Darius mutters. "You see, other universes all *look* exactly like this one. At first, anyway. But there's always one little difference. Usually a deadly difference."

You study his face. He sounds as if he knows what he's talking about. His words send a chill along your spine.

Turn to PAGE 136.

You stare at the horrible, terrifying *thing*. It has your eyes, your mouth, your hair. It's a shrunken version of you. You feel sick just looking at you.

"What . . . I mean how . . . ?" you whimper.

"Do you like it?" Uncle Darius asks. He smiles a nasty, teeth-baring smile.

Jamie grabs your arm. "Uh, w-w-we have to go now," she stammers. "We just remembered we have to study for a math test."

"I'm sure *you* don't need to study," Uncle Darius says to you. "Not with such a good head on your shoulders."

He raises one hand high. You gasp when you realize what he's holding. A gleaming, curved knife, almost as long as a sword.

You can't believe this is happening!

He takes a step forward and swings the knife — at your neck!

Should you duck and try to knock Darius over? Or run for the door?

Think fast. And try not to lose your head.

If you duck, turn to PAGE 85.
If you run, go to PAGE 102.

"Get them off me!" you howl. More and more bugs swarm onto you. They seem to *like* the spray. They gobble it up as if it were candy. You scream as they cover your shoes and pants in a seething, munching mass.

Jamie looks ill.

You glance down at the can. The words you read on the label make your heart leap into your throat.

BUGS LOVE OUR SPRAY! it says. IT'S THEIR FAVORITE TREAT! REMEMBER, BUGS ARE OUR FRIENDS. USE OUR SPRAY AND LOVE YOUR BUGS!

You keep spraying anyway. You hope if they get enough of the spray treat, they won't want to eat you!

But soon the spray is all gone.

And the bad news is, the bugs are still hungry. . . .

Doesn't that just bug you?

THE END

"I've got you!" Darius gloats.

Footsteps pound toward you. You don't waste time on a backwards glance. You simply fling open the door and dive through. Jamie slams it behind you and throws the bolt.

Darius pounds on the other side, but the door holds.

You made it!

"You think you're safe? Think again. You're trapped in there!" Darius shouts. "Stay as long as you like." He bellows with evil laughter.

"He's right," Jamie admits. "There's no way out except through that door."

You swallow hard. The basement is a dark pit below you, full of shadowy shapes.

But this is no time to panic.

Is it?

Find out on PAGE 25.

You decide to try boiling water. You and Jamie race to the kitchen. You each set two pots of water onto the stove and turn the heat on high. You pace back and forth until the water is bubbling. Then you carefully carry the heavy pots back into the lab.

"Ready?" Jamie asks.

You nod nervously, feeling imaginary little pinpricks of bug bites on your legs. You hope this works.

Jamie pushes the Transvator's door button with her foot.

As the doors open, the army of bugs surges toward you.

"Boil them!" Jamie shouts.

You tip the first pot onto the scurrying creatures. Hundreds are carried away by the wave of scalding water. *Yes!* You can hear their boiling bodies sizzle.

Jamie hurls both her pots of boiling water onto the Transvator walls. Masses of bugs wash down to the floor.

You dump your second pot on the few remaining insects. "We got them!" you cry.

"Let's get out of here!" Jamie yells.

You don't have to be told twice. Together you leap into the Transvator.

Go to PAGE 40.

Hey. There's no one in the lab!

You reach up and pull one of the earplugs out. You need to be able to hear. You don't want Darius sneaking up on you!

"Hey, Darius!" Jamie yells. "We want you to hear something."

You wait, trembling. But you don't hear a sound.

Jamie nudges you forward. You creep into the lab, imagining a huge machete swinging out of nowhere. The back of your neck tingles at the thought.

You point the Ear Irradicator into the dark lab. "Be careful — he could be anywhere," Jamie whispers behind you.

"I know," you snap. But she can't hear you.

You inch forward, swinging the Ear Irradicator from side to side.

Behind you Jamie lets out a gasp. You spin around.

It's Darius!

You fumble to put the earplug back into your unprotected ear. But you drop it!

Darius raises his machete — and throws it at your head!

If you're lucky, you'll duck in time.

How lucky are you?

Flip a coin. If you get heads, jump to PAGE 61. Tails? Tumble to PAGE 123.

10

You decide to push the button.

It looks a little like a stopwatch, after all. And you really wish this day would just stop!

You press the button. An unfamiliar voice starts to speak.

Hey. Maybe it's someone coming to save you!

"The time is three forty-one and forty seconds," the voice intones.

Great! A talking clock. That's a big help.

Headhunter Darius snickers. "Well, at least we know the exact time of death!"

He strides toward you, slashing the air with his machete.

Press another button — fast!

To press the 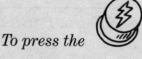 *button, go to PAGE 48.*

To press the 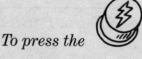 *button, go to PAGE 56.*

"Ouch!" Jamie cries as she hits the ground. The headhunters scramble over the fence in two seconds flat.

It takes you a few minutes to untangle Jamie from the barbed net, but the headhunters don't return. You guess you've seen the last of them.

"Good thinking!" Jamie congratulates you.

"I never shrink from a challenge," you joke.

Jamie groans. "Let's check out the shed," she suggests. "The real Uncle Darius might be trapped in there."

Uncle Darius! You forgot all about him!

Jamie opens the shed door and peers inside. "Can't see a thing," she mutters.

You both step inside. You feel along the wall for the light switch.

You don't find a switch. What you do find feels strangely familiar.

Then Jamie turns on the light.

Boy, do you wish she hadn't.

Feel your way to PAGE 79.

12

Gross! Mike's arms are covered with tiny bugs! They crawl in and out of his shirtsleeves. They scurry across the bare skin of his arms and neck.

The fabric of his shirt seems to ripple. You realize that the insects must be all over his body — a seething mass of scurrying little bodies. Your stomach heaves.

Mike stares at Jamie. Confusion replaces his glassy stare. "Something. Wrong?"

You grab her shoulder, trying to calm her down. She manages to stutter, "Uh, I . . ."

"What's. The. Matter?" a voice from behind you demands. "Don't. Like. Bugs?"

You turn around.

Uh-oh.

You're surrounded.

Go to PAGE 15.

You choose rock.

You thrust out a fist.

So does Jamie.

It's a tie!

"All right. One more time," she orders.

What should you do? Choose rock again — or pull a switch on Jamie?

Think fast!

If you choose rock again, turn to PAGE 132.

If you choose paper, turn to PAGE 121.

If you choose scissors, turn to PAGE 53.

EAU CLAIRE DISTRICT LIBRARY

"Jamie! Stop this thing!" you shout.

She clicks the remote frantically. "I'm trying!"

The robot lurches steadily toward you.

"On target. In motion," it repeats.

"Turn it off!" you scream.

"I did!" Jamie yells.

"Cannot turn off," the machine announces.

Oh.

Maybe you should have guessed that a robot made by a headhunter wouldn't want to go after a door. After all, doors don't have heads. Humans do.

You retreat and retreat. The robot is backing you into a corner. You throw a chair at it.

The machine's arms whirl. A moment later the chair is nothing more than a pile of toothpicks.

You start screaming. What's the point of trying to control yourself?

Any way you look at it, you're going to pieces!

THE END

Jamie's scream must have alerted the neighbors. They stand in a tight circle around you.

At first glance they all seem normal. There are three kids and two men wearing regular clothes. The kids hold skateboards. One man holds a rake, the other a newspaper.

But their faces send a chill down your spine. They all have the same waxy skin. They stare at you with narrowed and suspicious eyes.

They're peering at you. Trying to figure something out.

Your arms, you realize. They're staring at your arms.

One question.

Are you wearing long sleeves or short?

If you're wearing short sleeves, go to PAGE 39.
If you're wearing long sleeves, go to PAGE 17.

You grab the machete. Then you bolt back down the hall and peer out the window.

Uh-oh. They're lifting Jamie over the fence.

You've got to act now!

Taking a deep breath, you fling open the door and hurl yourself toward the headhunters.

"Ahhhhhhh!"

Their heads whip around at your bloodcurdling scream.

And you fight pretty well, for someone who's never used a machete before. And who's outnumbered five to one.

Five to one? Never used a machete before?

What were you thinking?

A headhunter knocks your machete out of your grasp. Whoops! Looks like you forgot — these people are experts! They grew up with machetes in their hands!

Guess you didn't use your head.

And you know what they say:

Use it or lose it!

THE END

You realize that the neighbors are checking to see if there are bugs on your arms.

Luckily, your shirt has long sleeves. So does Jamie's.

"No. Problem," Jamie chants. "We. Like. Bugs." She elbows you in the ribs.

You get it. You try to make your eyes go blank. "Yes. Bugs. Good," you agree.

All the neighbors smile. "Bugs. Are. Friends," they chant.

They turn back toward their houses. Gross! Little insect antennae poke out of sleeves and over collars. You can barely keep from gagging.

The moment the neighbors are out of earshot, Jamie mutters, "What is with these people? They act like zombies. I think the bugs are controlling them."

The thought of bugs running the whole world makes your skin crawl. But it's not your problem, is it?

It's not even your universe!

"Let's get out of here," you whisper. "This place bugs me out!"

Go to PAGE 34.

"Uncle Darius!" Jamie cries.

That's right. It's the nice Uncle Darius — the one from *your* universe.

"Are we glad to see you!" you blurt out.

"Good to see you too," he exclaims. "Now get me out of this contraption — before it shrinks my head!"

You made it in time!

You and Jamie pull Darius from the machine. "I'm glad you found me. Good work!" he declares. "How did you do it?"

"With a little help from the Captivator Helmet and your head-hunting double," you explain, glowing with pride.

"I'm glad someone is using my inventions for a good purpose," Darius comments as he leads you back to the Transvator. "You've earned some extra help on your science fair project."

"Science fair project!" You groan. You forgot all about it! The afternoon is almost gone, and you haven't even started!

"We're doomed," Jamie mumbles. "It's due tomorrow."

"If only we could explain what happened." You sigh. "But no one would ever believe us."

Jamie's eyes light up. "Unless they *had* to believe us!"

Turn to PAGE 111.

The bugs start to swarm out of the Transvator.

"Shut the door!" Jamie screams.

You stab the button frantically as the insects scurry toward you. The doors slide closed.

You and Jamie stomp desperately on the bugs around you. You crush most of the scurrying little creatures. But you feel the sting of a few bites on your ankles.

You pull up the cuffs of your pants. And shudder.

Some of the bugs cling to your skin. You wince with disgust as you pluck them off one by one. It seems to take forever.

"You got only a few bites," Jamie declares, glancing at your ankles. "We're lucky the Transvator doors closed so fast."

A strange peaceful feeling washes over you. "Bites. Not. A. Problem," you say.

That's funny, you think. Why am I talking so slowly?

Feels. Good. Though.

Jamie stares at you with alarm. She grabs your shoulders.

"Hey!" she shouts. "Don't turn into a bug-zombie on me!"

"Don't. Worry. Feel. Fine," you reply.

Go. To. PAGE. 21.

"Take us to Uncle Darius. Now!" Jamie commands.

Darius trudges into the lab. You follow him into the Transvator. He punches some buttons on the wall.

You gulp. Are you really going to another universe?

A universe full of headhunters?

The Transvator rattles and shakes. The lights flicker.

Finally the machine quiets down. When the doors slide open, you peer out nervously.

The room looks a lot like the lab you were just in. But the inventions are all tools for head-hunting. And head-shrinking!

Whoa. You *have* gone to a parallel universe!

"Take us to Uncle Darius," Jamie repeats.

Darius plods ahead of you. He leads you to a door with a big KEEP OUT sign on it.

"Open it," you order.

Darius reaches for the door, but his hand falters as he touches the knob. What's wrong?

Then you realize he's staring at the KEEP OUT sign. Wow! He can't even disobey a sign!

Should you tell him to take it off? Or take it off yourself? Either way, he's not going through that door until the sign comes down.

To tell Darius to take it off, turn to PAGE 133.
To take it off yourself, turn to PAGE 68.

Jamie drags you from the lab. She forces you through the bathroom door and shoves you into the shower.

"Have. Clothes. On. Still," you murmur. What is she doing?

Then she turns on the cold water, full blast.

"Yeeeoow!" you shriek. The freezing water jolts you like ice cubes raining onto your back. You leap from the shower.

"Are you okay now?" Jamie asks.

You glare at her, furious. Then you realize what almost happened. "I-I was turning into a bug-zombie!" you sputter.

"I know!" Jamie answers. "It must be the bites that do it. At least you only got a few. Imagine what it's like to have all those things living on you, day and night!"

You shudder at the thought. Too horrible!

"And now the Transvator is full of them," Jamie wails. "How are we going to get out of here?"

"Let's try to find some bug spray," you suggest.

Jamie frowns. "Why would they even *have* bug spray in this universe? Bugs. Are. Friends. Remember?"

You scratch your head. "Well, maybe —"

Then the sound of a screaming siren drowns you out.

Go to PAGE 95.

You twist and squirm, trying to escape. But Mr. Johnson clutches your hair even tighter. You gulp as his knife blade sparkles in the sun.

The other hunters rush forward. They pin your arms to your sides as Mr. Johnson raises his machete higher.

"You never were too bright, were you?" Mr. Johnson sneers. "But cheer up. You're about to become the head of your class!"

THE END

You decide to pull the DENTIST'S DRILL trigger.

Nothing could be worse than the sound of a metal screw boring into your teeth!

You pull the trigger. The lab fills with the horrible, screeching whine of a drill.

Even with one ear plugged, it feels as if there's a whirling drill in your own mouth. You can actually feel your teeth vibrate.

Darius writhes on the floor, his hands covering his mouth protectively. The noise is so awful that you can barely hold down the trigger. But you manage.

Finally you can't stand it anymore. You release the trigger.

The noise stops.

Darius seems to be knocked out cold!

Drill your way to PAGE 92.

You press the button labeled FLIP. You have no idea what it means.

You're about to find out.

The lights inside the Transvator flicker and go dim. A deep rumble comes through the soles of your feet. It grows louder.

"Is it supposed to make this noise?" you ask nervously.

"I don't know," Jamie murmurs. "Maybe it's broken."

Great. Just what you wanted to hear. Not.

The Transvator shakes as the rumbling noise grows even louder. You and Jamie have to hold on to each other to keep from falling over.

But finally the Transvator shudders and is still.

Jamie reaches toward the DOOR OPEN button. "Ready?"

"As I'll ever be," you reply.

She pushes the button.

The doors slide open.

Hmmm.

"What's wrong with this picture?" Jamie asks.

Open to PAGE 134.

Jamie turns on the lights. You peer down into the basement.

Like the lab, it's crowded with all kinds of devices and mechanical parts. But everything appears old and dusty.

"Does any of this stuff even work?" you ask.

Jamie looks worried. "I hope so."

You push aside cobwebs as you rummage through the junk.

"Hey, here's a pair of Escalator Shoes," Jamie calls. "They lift you right off the ground. Maybe we could attack Darius from above!" She frowns. "At least, I think that's how they work."

"Sounds good. What's this?" You hold up a dented metal hat.

"Captivator Helmet. Whoever wears it is under the control of your mind," Jamie explains.

Hmmm. Could be useful. But how would you get it onto Darius's head — without losing your own?

You also find something labeled EAR IRRADICA-TOR. Jamie isn't sure, but she thinks it's supposed to make terrible noises.

"Terrible enough to drive Darius out of this universe?" you ask.

Jamie shrugs. You stare at each other, stumped. Which invention should you try?

To use the Escalator Shoes, go to PAGE 37.
To use the Ear Irradicator, go to PAGE 57.
To use the Captivator Helmet, go to PAGE 78.

You decide to say something. When will you ever have another chance to have a conversation with a cat?

"Hi," you say. "We're from another universe. Do you have any headhunters here?"

Jamie glances at you, one eyebrow raised.

Okay, so it wasn't the most brilliant opening sentence.

Now it's the animals' turn to be shocked. Sapphire sits up straight. The dog's ears flatten on its head.

"We're searching for my uncle Darius," Jamie adds.

"That Transvator of yours has done something to them," the dog growls. "They're monsters!"

"We're not monsters," Jamie argues. "Just people."

"People who talk!" the dog barks. "It's horrible!"

"I think it's very interesting," Sapphire exclaims. "And I think they could be valuable."

Valuable? You don't like the sound of that.

Sapphire leaps up onto a worktable and pokes through the inventions. She selects a cruel-looking device from the table. It resembles a small harpoon gun, like the ones sea divers use.

She lifts it with her paws and aims. Right at you.

Go to PAGE 115.

You'd rather try to capture the evil, head-hunting Uncle Darius.

"I don't want to go to any other universes," you explain. "Especially a universe where *my* head is someone else's paperweight!"

"We need a weapon, then," Jamie says. "Let's take a look in the basement. That's where Uncle Darius keeps his old inventions."

You creep out of the library, trying not to make a sound.

Halfway down the hall you pass a closet. A bright red sign on it reads DANGER — DISINTE-GRATOR CLOSET.

"Hey, Jamie," you whisper. "What's this thing?"

"Uncle Darius told me never to play with that," she whispers back. "It's really dangerous! Come on — let's keep going."

"So are headhunters!" you argue. "I say we try to lure Darius in there. We can threaten to disintegrate him. That'll teach him!"

What do you think? Lure Darius into the Disintegrator Closet? Or head down to the basement for another invention?

To use the Disintegrator Closet, turn to PAGE 45.

To go to the basement, crawl to PAGE 72.

Your own name is on that empty box!

Then you remember. In this universe you've been "collected" too.

You and Jamie cautiously explore the rest of the house. Everything you find makes you glad you don't belong in this universe.

There are booby traps for catching victims. Electric saws and machete sharpeners for head removal. Even vats of pickling juice for shrinking the heads.

But no Uncle Darius.

Jamie peers through a window. "There's a shed out back," she notes. "Maybe that's where the head-hunting Darius put the real Darius."

"Or maybe he's down there," you suggest, pointing at the basement door. The door has a heavy padlock on it and a big KEEP OUT sign.

"How do we get in there?" Jamie asks.

You consider the possibilities. You could search the house for the key to the padlock. Or check out the backyard shed.

But going outside in this universe makes you nervous.

Time to use your head. What should you do?

To check out the backyard shed, turn to PAGE 46.

To look for a key to the basement, search for PAGE 126.

You decide to search the house for a weapon.

Jamie checks the closets while you search the kitchen. You brace yourself as you open each cupboard, wondering if a swarm of bugs waits for you inside.

You jump when Jamie bounds into the room. "Look what I found!" she shouts. She holds out a can labeled BUG SPRAY.

"Cool!" you exclaim. Then you scratch your head. "But I thought you said they wouldn't have bug spray in this universe."

Jamie shrugs her shoulders. "Well, they do." She puts the spray on the counter.

"Maybe we should use something else," you say uneasily.

"Like what?" Jamie asks.

You glance around the kitchen. Your eyes stop at the stove. "Boiling water!" you exclaim. "We could cook the bugs alive!"

"If we can get them all on the first shot," Jamie points out. She frowns. "I'm not sure what to do. I get the feeling we'll only get one try. What do *you* think?"

To try the bug spray, turn to PAGE 42.
To use boiling water, go to PAGE 8.

30

"Run for it!" Jamie shouts. She tears out of the bushes and into the backyard.

You follow her down the block, cutting through backyards, climbing fences, and dodging around swimming pools.

Sirens blare from all directions. You know you're being chased, but you don't dare glance back.

"This way," Jamie calls. She dashes through a gap in a chain-link fence at the end of the block. Huge, boarded-up warehouse buildings loom in front of you. "We can hide in these old abandoned factories," she pants.

You follow Jamie to one of the gigantic buildings. You sneak in through a broken door. In the sudden darkness you stumble over a loose board.

At least you don't hear any footsteps behind you. The sirens all seem far away now.

You shiver in the musty air. "This place gives me the creeps," you admit. "I wonder how long it's been since anyone's been in here."

"Don't move!" a voice commands from the shadows.

Okay, but how are you going to turn to PAGE 58?

"No!" you gasp. "No!"

Two Dariuses grin at you from inside the closet!

"You idiot. You duplicated him!" Jamie shrieks.

You reach to slam the door shut again.

Too late. The two Dariuses burst out into the hall. One grabs you by the arms. The other grabs Jamie. They throw you both against the wall.

Then they thrust both their machetes against *your* throat.

Why me? you wonder. Why not Jamie?

You don't have to wait long for your answer.

"Now we can complete our collection!" One Darius snickers.

"We'll have a matching pair!" the other cackles.

Well, at least *they're* happy.

Sure, they are. After all, two heads are better than one!

THE END

You stare at the lettering on the side of the van:

ANTI-CHILD PATROL
TO REPORT LOOSE KIDS,
CALL 1-800-NO-CHILD

Anti-child patrol? What kind of universe is this?

The police remove your handcuffs — the handcuffs that started out as toys. They throw you into the back of the van. The doors slam, leaving you and Jamie in total darkness.

"Can you believe it?" you sputter. "Whoever heard of a place where kids are illegal?"

Jamie's voice is sad. "And the Uncle Darius in this universe invents toys to catch them."

"I take it back about wanting to live here," you mutter.

"You may wind up living here," Jamie comments. "Unless we can escape from this van."

Yikes! You and Jamie feel around the van in the darkness.

"I found the door handle," Jamie whispers. "Do you have anything I can use to pick the lock?"

Well, do you?

Check your pockets or your backpack for a paper clip or pen.

If you have one with you, go to PAGE 60.

If not, turn to PAGE 63.

You're still trying to process the idea of a talking cat when another voice chimes in. "I don't know why you bother."

You gulp when you see the source of the voice. It's a big black dog!

"You know they can't understand you," the dog declares. "They're just stupid humans."

"Well, they can understand the tone of my voice," Sapphire protests. "And you can see from their faces that they know I'm very, *very* angry!"

A trickle of sweat runs down your back.

This is a different universe all right. A very weird one!

Maybe you should just step back into the nice Transvator and go somewhere else.

Or should you say something to the cat?

What would you say to a cat, anyway? Good kitty?

Think fast, though. Cats hate it when humans can't make up their minds.

To talk to the animals, go to PAGE 26.

To jump back into the Transvator, go to PAGE 91.

You and Jamie head back to Darius's house. You walk slowly, careful not to make the zombie neighbors suspicious. If they find out you're not bug infested, you don't know what they'll do.

You shudder with relief when you get inside the house. As Jamie strides ahead of you down the hall, you catch yourself peering into all the dark corners.

Are those little insect heads you see staring back at you?

No way. It must be your imagination, you tell yourself.

You and Jamie reach the lab. You rush up to the Transvator and press the OPEN DOOR button.

"I'll be glad to get out of this universe," you declare.

"You said it," Jamie agrees.

The doors *swoosh* open.

Oh, no.

The walls of the Transvator squirm and ripple. They're covered with thousands of bugs!

Head to PAGE 19.

A tiny, shrunken person glares up at you from the bottom of the bag.

Mr. Johnson! The evil, head-hunting Mr. Johnson. The one you sprayed with that red goo.

"Just a little something you picked up?" you joke.

Jamie laughs. "A tiny reminder of our trip to another universe. The real Mr. Johnson is in for a shock!"

You close the bag and tuck it under your arm. "You know," you tell Jamie, "I have a feeling this is going to be the best science fair ever!"

"Yeah. But don't let it go to your head!" Jamie replies.

THE END

You decide to try to talk your way out. After all, you don't even know what the Kid Test is. It could be dangerous!

"See, we're from another universe," you begin.

The leader of the Truants stares at you as if you're nuts.

You take a deep breath. "I know it sounds crazy, but it's true. And in our universe, kids aren't illegal," you go on.

You explain about video games and movies made just for kids. You can see some of the Truant kids getting interested.

"And there are special holidays when kids get tons of presents," Jamie adds.

"Wow!" someone exclaims.

Soon the Truants are hanging on every word. "How can we go to your universe?" the littlest kid asks.

"We have a Transuniversal Transvator," you answer.

"My uncle Darius invented it," Jamie chimes in.

At his name, a hiss goes through the room.

"Darius!" the leader shouts. "He's the one who invented trap toys!"

Just then a siren sounds outside.

"The police!" the leader cries. He whirls and points at you and Jamie. "They *are* spies! Grab them!"

Try talking your way out of this one on PAGE 130.

You choose the Escalator Shoes. Actually, you're psyched to try them out. You've always wanted to fly!

You strap them to your feet. They're huge. Almost as big as ski boots. Then you grab a heavy wrench that's hanging on the wall.

"What are you going to do?" Jamie asks.

"I'm going to fly up and bop Darius on the head from above," you explain. "He'll never know what hit him!"

"I don't know about this," Jamie cautions. "I have a feeling there's some kind of trick to those shoes."

"Like what?" you challenge.

"I don't know," Jamie admits.

You wave a hand. "Relax. I'll be fine."

You're not afraid to try the shoes, even if she is.

Fly ahead to PAGE 43.

When you wake up, you're in a metal cage.

A few animals gaze at you and Jamie from the other side of the bars. When you ask what's going on, they're happy to explain.

You're in the National Human Zoo. Probably the best zoo in the world!

"But we're human beings!" you protest. "I mean, we're *intelligent* humans! We can talk!"

The lion zookeeper nods his shaggy head happily at this. You're bound to be the most popular exhibit they've had in years!

Once you learn a few tricks, that is. . . .

THE END

One of the men points at your bare arms. "Look. No. Bugs."

Suddenly they all start to shiver. Their clothes bulge and ripple. As if a million little bodies are pushing to get out.

And onto you!

"Let's get out of here!" Jamie screams.

You lunge toward a gap in the circle of neighbors. Jamie darts through next to you. You take off.

The buggy neighbors shout for you to stop.

You just hope they run as slowly as they talk!

You tear across Uncle Darius's lawn. Jamie beats you to the front door. You're about to leap through after her — when a pair of strong hands grabs you from behind. Mike!

"Let me go!" you shout. You twist and squirm, trying to free yourself from Mike's grip.

Oh, no! The other neighbors grab you too.

You catch a last glimpse of Jamie disappearing into the house. You hope she makes it.

Then you feel a tickling sensation on the back of your neck. . . .

Squirm your way to PAGE 87.

All the buttons in the Transvator look the same — except that some of them have handwritten labels next to them.

Unfortunately, the labels don't make any sense. You hesitate.

Which button should you push?

If you push FAUNA, *turn to* PAGE 76.
If you push FLIP, *turn to* PAGE 24.
If you push TRAPPER, *turn to* PAGE 73.
If you push BUGGY, *turn to* PAGE 93.
If you push TRUANTS, *turn to* PAGE 47.

You and Jamie follow Uncle Darius into the Transvator. He works the controls expertly. Soon the machine is groaning and shaking its way back to your universe.

The noise rises to a roar — then stops. The lights go out.

When they come back on, Uncle Darius has a normal-size head again! "Ah, that's better," he booms in his old voice.

You're glad to be home at last. But you're also petrified.

"So what do we do now?" Jamie asks. She sounds as scared as you feel.

"Don't worry," Uncle Darius says. "I have a secret weapon!"

He pulls a little device out of his pocket. "I can use this control box to work all the inventions in my house. There are two hundred and forty-seven different gadgets in the lab alone. *Something* should get the job done!"

You hope he's right.

Because headhunter Darius is waiting just beyond the Transvator doors.

The doors open with a *whoosh*.

Go to PAGE 109, if you dare.

You decide to use the bug spray. After all, bug spray is bug spray. Right?

You grab the spray can and hurry into the lab. Jamie reaches to push the Transvator OPEN DOOR button.

"Wait!" you cry. "What if the bugs come out too quickly to spray them all?"

"Spray your shoes and pants legs," Jamie suggests. "That should keep them off."

Great idea! You hit the nozzle. Stinky, sticky stuff covers your cuffs. It smells so bad, it has to work!

"Okay, ready," you announce.

Jamie pushes the button. The doors whoosh open.

Thousands of bugs stream out toward you. You squeeze the nozzle, coating them with spray.

But they're not stopping!

"Uh-oh," Jamie says in a weird voice. "Oh, no!" she cries. "I don't think 'bug spray' means the same thing in this universe as it does in ours!"

Go to PAGE 6.

"Don't worry about me," you assure her. "With these shoes, our troubles will be over in no time. Just open the door for me."

Shrugging, Jamie climbs the stairs and waits by the door.

You bend down and press the START buttons on the shoes.

You feel a hum building in the soles. Your feet feel a little warm. Then something incredible happens. . . .

You lift into the air!

"Cool!" you shout.

Your feet hover a few inches from the floor. It's as if you're walking on some invisible surface.

You point your toes at the stairs and float up toward the basement door. "Coming through!" you announce.

Jamie throws open the door. You soar into the hall, brandishing the wrench. You're about two feet off the floor by now.

Darius is nowhere in sight.

You grin. He must be hiding. He probably knows he's a goner!

You zoom toward the lab.

"Wait!" Jamie calls after you. "I just remembered something about those shoes!"

Rise to PAGE 112.

"I guess if we rescue your uncle Darius, he could help us with this crazy headhunter," you say.

"Or we could try to capture *this* Uncle Darius," Jamie suggests. "And make him take us back to his universe. Then he could show us where the real Uncle Darius is!"

"Capture him? How?" you demand.

"We could use one of the inventions that are lying around the house," Jamie explains. "There are lots of cool things."

You shake your head in confusion. This is turning out to be much more complicated than any science project. And a lot more dangerous!

If you stay here, you'll have to face a knife-wielding maniac who wants your head. But if you try to find help in another universe, who knows what you'll find?

Should you try to capture the evil Darius using the inventions in the house? Or would you rather head for the Transvator to try and rescue the real Uncle Darius?

Take the Transvator on PAGE 77.
Try to capture the evil Darius on PAGE 27.

You decide to lure Darius into the Disintegrator Closet. You even have a foolproof plan.

"Get Darius to chase you back here," you whisper to Jamie. "And I'll push him into the closet as he runs past."

Jamie scowls. "Why do I get to be the bait?"

"Who runs faster? You or me?" you demand.

"Me. You've got a point. I guess," she mutters.

You position yourself in the bathroom across from the closet. You're glad Darius's house is so dark. There's no way he'll see you before you push him into the closet!

Jamie walks down the hall, then pretends to trip and fall.

"Ow! My leg!" she cries, writhing on the floor as if in pain. "Help me! Quick!"

Headhunter Darius's laughter rolls through the house. "I'm coming," he calls. "Don't worry about a thing!"

Heavy footsteps pound the floor. Peeking out of the bathroom, you see a shadowy form at the end of the hall.

Jamie jumps up. Still pretending to be hurt, she limps away from him. You gulp, preparing to leap.

Darius charges after her. She picks up speed.

Just as Darius runs by the bathroom, you leap out.

Leap onto PAGE 94.

46

You decide to venture into the backyard. You don't tell Jamie — but you want to get away from that empty glass box with your name on it.

The bright sunlight makes you feel very exposed — especially after the darkness of Darius's house. You're glad there are high fences between you and the neighbors. You can't see anybody.

You hope nobody can see you, either!

You and Jamie steal across the backyard. The shed is just a few steps in front of you.

But then Jamie screams.

Turn to PAGE 101.

You hit the button labeled TRUANTS.

The Transvator starts to rumble and shiver. Then, with a *whoosh,* it shoots *sideways!*

"Wait! Where are we going?" Jamie cries.

"Don't know," you shout back.

When the Transvator finally stops, you and Jamie step out. You peer into Darius's lab. Are you really in a different universe? What will you find here?

Right away you notice the inventions are different. Instead of huge, weird machines, the room is full of radio-controlled airplanes, model rockets, toy train sets, and the biggest collection of action figures you've ever seen!

"Cool toys!" you exclaim, reaching for one.

"Hold on," Jamie cries. "We don't know anything about this universe. Those toys could be a trap. Let's find Uncle Darius."

You peer at the toys. They don't seem dangerous.

"Well, maybe we can find out something about this universe by checking out the toys," you suggest.

Should you take a quick look at the toys? Or try to find Darius now?

To check out the toys, turn to PAGE 131.
To look for Uncle Darius, turn to PAGE 110.

You press the button.

The instant you do, all the lights go out. You can't see a thing!

"Think I can't find you in the dark?" Darius taunts. "We'll just see about that."

Then you hear a terrible sound. The swish of his machete whistling through the air. He's swinging it back and forth as he moves through the dark.

He's heading straight toward you. With no hesitation.

It's as if he can see in the dark!

You drop to your knees and crawl away. Your heart is pounding.

Maybe headhunter Darius will fall into the pit in the darkness, you think hopefully.

Instead, a hand darts out and closes around your wrist.

"Got you," headhunter Darius declares triumphantly.

See the light on PAGE 86.

In the basement is a machine that shrinks heads. While the victim is still alive!

The nice Uncle Darius is attached to the machine. His head is *very* tiny. You stare at it blankly.

When he speaks, it sounds just like a mouse squeaking. Too bad. It sounds as if he wants you to do something. But his voice is too high and shrill. You can't understand a word he says.

"Just stand here," head-hunting Darius commands.

You stand still while he hooks you up to the machine. He attaches electrodes and tubes to your head.

He takes off your helmet. Then he flips a switch.

Suddenly you remember. You don't want your head shrunk!

"Let me go!" you shout.

But it's too late.

Who's going to listen to someone with a squeaky little voice like yours?

THE END

You think you've got it. "The Cuckoo Clock of Doom made you older and older," you announce. "Right?"

"Wrong!" the leader yells. "You're no kid!"

The Truants grab you and Jamie and hold you down.

"We're going to make sure you never betray any kids again," the leader announces.

One of the older kids produces a strange-looking pen. It makes a whirring sound. He bends over you.

And starts to write on your face!

You struggle, but you can't move. Finally it's over. The leader holds a mirror up to your face.

The words are backwards in the mirror. You stare at them:

ɿoɟis𝟋T
oɟ
ꙅbiꓘ

You try to wipe the writing off.

"I'm afraid that's permanent," the leader snickers.

You glance over at Jamie. She has the same thing written on her face. Except it's easier to read: TRAITOR TO KIDS.

Sirens suddenly blare outside. The police!

Turn to PAGE 129.

You decide to let Jamie switch on the robot. But you stand as far away as you can, on the other side of the basement door.

Jamie studies the remote control for a moment. Then she selects a button and points the remote at the robot.

Click! Whirrr!

The robot comes to life. A motor whines as a big wheel in the robot's middle starts rolling. The robot scrapes each cutting tool against the wheel. A shower of sparks fills the hall.

"Look," Jamie gasps, "it's sharpening itself!"

The scraping sound makes your teeth ache.

Finally the robot finishes sharpening its knives. A mechanical voice comes out of it. "Awaiting orders."

Jamie licks her lips and presses another button on the remote. "I think this will make it cut through the basement door," she tells you.

"On target," the robot croaks. "Moving now."

It heads your way. You step back. You don't want to be anywhere nearby when those blades start to cut.

The robot reaches the basement door — and glides past it.

Right toward you!

"On target. In motion," it bleats happily.

Aim toward PAGE 14.

You make it back to the doorway with aching arms. Jamie reaches out and pulls you in.

"I didn't like the scenery," you comment shakily.

"Why not? It looked like a nice *fall* day to me," Jamie declares.

"Ha-ha," you mutter.

She is just *too* smart sometimes.

Now you have to get back inside the Transvator. You take a deep breath and try Jamie's handstand maneuver.

All right! You do it perfectly.

"Ta-da!" you cry.

Return to PAGE 40.

You choose scissors.

Then you see that Jamie's hand is curled in a fist.

You force a smile. "So — scissors cut everything, right?"

"Not rocks," Jamie retorts. "Put on the helmet."

You frown. "Okay, but don't make me do anything stupid."

"You mean, nothing more stupid than what you usually do," she answers, laughing.

"Ha-ha," you grumble.

You pick up the helmet and put it on. It feels itchy for a moment, like there are spiders crawling around in your hair. You start to pull it off.

But then your mind goes blank.

What was I doing? you wonder. I need someone to tell me what to do!

Jamie stares at you strangely.

"Put your hands in the air," she suggests.

Sure. Whatever. You put them up.

That's nice.

"All right." Jamie grins. "Now say that you're a big doofus."

There's nothing wrong with saying that, is there?

Turn to PAGE 127.

54

You decide to run for the house.

As you race toward the back door, a headhunter throws another net toward you. You hit the ground.

The net flies over you and wraps itself around another headhunter. He screams as the hooks bite into him.

You scramble to your feet and fling yourself through the door. You slam it shut behind you and lock it.

Safe!

But they've still got Jamie. You've got to help her!

You tear down the hall to the lab. The clutter of strange devices confuses you. You don't know what any of them are for!

One catches your eye. It looks sort of like a paint sprayer. But knowing how this universe works, you figure it doesn't spray paint. Probably some kind of poison gas!

You also spot an extra-long machete. One with *two* blades instead of one.

That should put a scare into the headhunters!

Which should you grab? The sprayer or the machete?

Think fast — or Jamie's headed for the display case.

To use the sprayer, go to PAGE 83.
To use the machete, cut straight to PAGE 16.

Ms. Jay appears in the window of her house. She's staring out at you and talking frantically on the phone.

"Uh, maybe we should get back in the Transvator," you suggest nervously.

"Let's just hide in these bushes for a minute and see what happens," Jamie replies. "Maybe they want to head-hunt us."

"That's a *good* thing?" you exclaim.

"Sure." Jamie nods. "It means we're in the right universe to find Uncle Darius."

Great.

You hide in the dense bushes beside Darius's house. You're lucky his yard is overgrown in this universe too.

Soon a bunch of black cars pull up. A dozen police officers jump out and hurry into the house.

You huddle deeper into the bushes.

"Look at that," Jamie whispers. She points at the biggest of the police vehicles, a dark van with a caged rear window.

You gulp when you read the words on the side of the van.

Read them on PAGE 80.

56

You press the button.

A low hum fills the air. The lights flicker.

You glance around the lab, trying to figure out which of the 247 inventions you've triggered.

Then you spot a metal disk mounted high on a pole in the center of the room. The disk is starting to spin.

Headhunter Darius stares at the disk suspiciously, as if he's trying to figure out what it is.

You wish you knew.

The disk whirls faster and faster. The hum builds into a high-pitched scream. The disk seems to crackle with electricity.

Evil Darius shrugs and steps toward you. "These toys don't scare me!" he scoffs.

The hum grows louder as the disk spins faster.

Why doesn't it *do* anything? you wonder.

Darius strides closer, gripping his machete.

Your heart thumps in double time. You feverishly punch all the buttons on the remote.

None of them seems to work! Nothing happens.

Darius is inches away. He raises his machete high.

Only a miracle can save you now!

Find out if there's a miracle on PAGE 81.

"Time for something drastic," you declare.

You grab the Ear Irradicator.

It looks like an old-fashioned gun. But instead of a regular barrel, it ends in a wide opening, like the mouth of a trumpet.

You aim it at Jamie. "Pow!" you yell. You grin.

"Be careful with that!" she shouts. "Don't shoot it until we put in these earplugs." She hands you two gummy wads of wax.

You shove the wads into your ears. Then you study the Ear Irradicator more closely.

Weird. It has three triggers. Each is labeled.

You squint at the tiny writing next to each trigger.

One label says FINGERNAILS ON CHALKBOARD. Another says DRIPPING FAUCET. The last says DENTIST'S DRILL.

Those all sound pretty irritating!

Jamie says something, but you can't hear her with your earplugs in. "What?" you shout.

Whoa. You can't even hear yourself!

Jamie points toward the stairs. You follow her up to the door. She unlocks the bolt.

You raise the weapon with trembling hands.

Then Jamie kicks open the door.

Take a peek on PAGE 9.

"Put your hands on your head," the voice commands.

You and Jamie obey. Your heart starts pounding. It looks as if you've been caught by the Anti-Child Patrol after all.

Then someone steps out of the shadows.

It's a kid! Just about your age.

He's dirty and his clothes are ragged, but when he speaks, he sounds as if he's used to giving orders.

"Are you working for *them?*" he demands.

"W-w-who?" you stammer.

"The grownups, of course!" He looks disgusted.

You hear muttering all around you. Now that your eyes are adjusting, you see that the abandoned factory is full of children. They're all filthy and tangle-haired.

"No," Jamie insists. "The police were chasing us!"

The leader looks you over. "Well, you *look* like real kids. But they've sent spies to catch us Truants before." He studies you thoughtfully. "We'll see if you can pass the Kid Test."

Test? You're terrible at tests!

Should you take the Kid Test — whatever that is? Or should you try to talk your way out of this?

Take the Kid Test on PAGE 106.
Try talking your way out on PAGE 36.

You decide to feel around for the light switch. After all, you've already held hands with a headless corpse. What could be worse than that?

Nothing.

Right?

You wince as your hand creeps along the wall. What horrible things could be hanging on a headhunter's basement wall? you wonder.

Then you touch it.

Touch what? Find out on PAGE 114.

60

You hand Jamie the tool you found.

She works at the lock, muttering under her breath.

You realize your hands are sweating. You don't want to stay trapped in this anti-kid universe! "Hurry!" you plead.

"Got it!" Jamie cries.

The door springs open. "Whoa!" you exclaim. You blink in the sudden light. The scenery rushes past outside.

Then the van stops for a red light. "Go!" you cry. You and Jamie jump to the ground.

All around you, car horns start to honk.

"Runaway children!" someone yells. "Get them!"

The front doors of the van open. Police officers pile out. Fortunately, you're next to a big park. You run for the trees.

As fast as you can, you and Jamie make your way back to Uncle Darius's house.

"Now what?" Jamie pants as you dash inside.

You don't even have to think about it. You've had enough of this universe!

"Into the Transvator!" you cry, leading the way.

Transvate yourself to PAGE 40.

The long knife hurtles toward you, flipping end over end. It seems to be moving in slow motion.

You throw yourself to one side, but it feels as if *you're* moving in slow motion too.

You can tell you aren't going to make it.

Heads was not a lucky flip this time.

Because you're about to lose yours!

THE END

62

"And to think I didn't even want you as a science project partner!" Jamie exclaims. "We make a great team. We rescued my uncle from another universe and defeated a crazed killer, all in one afternoon."

She's right. You do make a great team. Wait until you and Jamie tell the kids at school tomorrow about all the stuff that happened to you. They'd never believe *you*, but with Jamie to back up your story, they'll *have* to.

But then a terrible thought strikes you.

"Sunday afternoon is almost gone," you complain. "And we haven't even started our science project. It's due tomorrow!"

"Oh, I'll help you with that," Uncle Darius booms. "I've got a million ideas. Let me just demonstrate one of my new inventions. . . ."

You and Jamie exchange a terrified look.

Take a look on PAGE 116.

You don't have anything for Jamie to use to pick the lock. There's no way to escape the van.

So you wait. "When the van stops, we'll make a run for it," you tell Jamie.

Finally you come to a halt. The doors swing open.

"Now!" you scream, leaping from the van.

But you don't get very far. There's nowhere to go.

You're surrounded by towering gray stone walls.

"Welcome to The School," a police officer says. She holds Jamie in a tight grip. Another officer grabs your arm.

Your heart sinks as they lead you inside. "Cheer up," one of the officers chuckles. "School is fun! You'll love it. You'd better. Because you're here until your eighteenth birthday."

Looks like you won't be saving Uncle Darius any time soon.

But don't worry, you won't be bored. School in this universe runs seven days a week, eighteen hours a day. And there's tons of homework. And no recess. Ever.

But you don't mind. School is fun!

Right?

THE END

"Ow!" you complain, rubbing your arm. "I liked you better as a mindless robot."

"That's because only a mindless robot would say that you're smarter than I am," Jamie retorts.

"If —" you start to say. Then you break off as an idea hits you.

"I am smarter than you," you reply smugly. "Because *I* have a brilliant plan for getting us out of this mess."

"What? Let's hear it!" Jamie cries.

"Okay. I'll hang from that beam over the door," you explain. "You lure Darius into the basement. When he comes in, I'll plop the helmet onto his head."

"You call that brilliant?" Jamie mutters.

But she climbs to the top of the stairs.

"Give me the helmet," she orders, swinging herself up onto the beam. "I'll do the hard part. All you have to do is get Darius in here — and stay out of the way of his machete."

You hand Jamie the helmet. Then, taking a deep breath, you slide back the bolt on the basement door.

You tense as the door creaks open.

A dark shadow looms in the doorway.

Turn to PAGE 98.

Mike's eyes stare straight through you and Jamie. His skin appears hard and shiny, almost as if he were made of wax.

"Hello. There. Jamie," Mike answers. The words come out choked and raspy.

You are *definitely* in a different universe, you decide. And this universe's version of Mike is really creepy!

Jamie takes a step back. She forces a smile. "Hey, Mike, how are you doing?" she asks.

"Feel. Great. All. Day. Every. Day." Mike smiles. But his smile appears as slowly and painfully as his words.

In your universe Mike is a fun guy. But you guess that in this universe, he's *not* the life of the party.

Mike gazes up at the high sun. "Warm. Today."

He takes off his jacket and throws it over his shoulder.

"Yaaaiiiieee!" Jamie screams.

You would too. But you're too horrified to make a sound.

See why on PAGE 12.

66

You're staring at a round metal contraption with more arms than you can count. Each one of them ends with a long, sharp cutting instrument. Some are machetes. Some are chain saws. Some you can't even identify.

"It's some kind of robot," Jamie answers.

"A very nasty kind," you observe.

"It's just a machine. But I bet it could cut through the basement door in about two seconds," Jamie declares.

"Or it could cut through us," you mutter.

"Relax. I have the remote control right here." She holds up a little box covered with buttons.

"But you don't know how it works," you argue.

"Do you have a better idea?" Jamie challenges.

You ponder this. *Any* idea must be better than switching on some sort of head-hunting robot. "Maybe we should check out the backyard shed first."

"I thought you were afraid of going outside," she taunts.

She's right. You were.

But you're also scared of this knife-wielding robot.

Which is worse? Leaving the house to check out the shed?

Or switching on the robot?

To check out the backyard shed, turn to PAGE 46.

To switch on the robot, go to PAGE 51.

You notice that Darius clutches some sort of remote control. He points it toward the door, and another set of bolts snaps shut.

"Remote control locks. Very handy." He cackles. "The Darius in this universe has some interesting hobbies."

He raises one arm. You can see the gleam of the long knife.

"But *my* hobbies are even more interesting," he declares.

You figure he's not talking about stamp collecting.

And you know what? You're right.

THE END

You rip down the sign. "Now open that door," you order.

Darius obeys, opening the door to a set of stairs leading down.

"Walk down the stairs," Jamie commands.

Darius plunges down the stairs into pitch darkness.

"Wait! Turn on a light first," you command.

He reaches for a light switch and flicks it to ON.

A huge explosion of sparks fills the air!

Turn to PAGE 117.

You decide to join the bug-zombies outside.

"Let's. Just. Be. Careful," Jamie cautions.

You gulp as you open the door. But none of the zombies glances at you when you join the line. It's as if they're all transfixed by the siren. You and Jamie shuffle along with them, trying not to show your fear.

You're thinking that this neighborhood is exactly like the one in your own universe. But then you reach the spot where the mall should be.

What you see is not a mall.

It's a statue in the shape of one of the bugs. Only this bug is *huge*. And it looks . . . hungry, somehow.

Long lines of people surround the statue. They walk one by one into its giant mouth.

You shudder. What are they doing in there?

You're starting to wonder if coming here was such a good idea.

Go to PAGE 99.

70

You decide to find a flashlight.

It doesn't take long. In fact, there's a flashlight hanging on a nail right next to the basement door. When you switch it on, you discover why Darius kept it handy.

The light switch is connected by naked wires to a huge fuse box labeled HIGH VOLTAGE.

A wave of nervous relief hits you. Clicking that switch would have been a shocking experience!

You and Jamie tread carefully down the stairs. You wonder what other tricks Darius hid down here.

Every footstep kicks a cloud of dust into the flashlight beam. The only sound is a dripping noise somewhere below.

At the bottom of the stairs you shine the flashlight on the only object in the basement — a huge refrigerator.

Drip. Drip. The sound comes from inside the refrigerator.

"I guess we have to open it," you mutter. You have a bad feeling about this.

"Yeah," Jamie agrees. She pulls the door open. What you see makes you feel cold all over.

Turn to PAGE 88.

"I-I-I must exist in that universe too," you stammer.

"You *used* to exist, you mean," Jamie corrects. "Until that evil Uncle Darius caught you and got your head."

"And now he wants a matching pair!" you cry.

"Shh!" Jamie warns. "He'll hear you."

"I'm getting out of here!" You start for the hallway.

"You can't," Jamie declares. "I already tried the door. It's locked. The controls are in the lab."

"Great!" you exclaim. "We're dead!"

"Not yet," Jamie answers. "We can try to get to the Transvator and go after Uncle Darius. The *real* Uncle Darius. We can rescue him."

A chill runs up your spine. "Go to the headhunter universe? That's crazy!"

"Would you rather stay *here?*" Jamie asks. "With him?"

You gulp, putting one hand to your throat. She has a point.

But all those headhunters will have a point too. At the end of their long, sharp head-hunting knives!

Turn to PAGE 44.

You decide to head down to the basement.

When you reach the end of the hall, Jamie puts her fingers against her lips in a silent *shh*. She points toward the lab.

You peer around the corner.

Yikes. Head-hunting Darius! He's pawing through the inventions and muttering to himself.

Just ahead of you is the basement door. But you'll have to cross through the lab to get there.

You turn to Jamie. "You first," you mouth.

Jamie nods. She drops to the floor and crawls silently behind the crowded tables. She reaches the basement door and nudges it open. Then she slips soundlessly inside.

Your turn.

You inch forward, trying not to make a sound.

Yes! You're at the door! You're going to make it!

Then a voice booms across the lab.

"Ah! There you are!"

Go to PAGE 7.

You stab at the button marked TRAPPER. You just hope that *you* don't get trapped.

The Transvator starts shaking even before your finger leaves the button. A low growling sound builds. You and Jamie clamp your hands over your ears.

The noise grows higher in pitch, until it sounds like some huge bird screaming as it dives for prey.

Finally the sound fades away. The Transvator comes to a trembling halt. The doors *whoosh* open.

You peer out into the dark lab. The inventions don't look exactly... friendly. You spot a bear trap with giant steel jaws.

Whoa. This definitely isn't the same lab you were in a few seconds ago.

Jamie takes a few cautious steps forward.

"Uncle Darius?" she calls down the dark hallway.

You follow her down the hall toward the library. The warm light of reading lamps spills out into the hall.

But when Jamie steps into the library, she stops short.

"I think we found the right universe," she whispers.

When you step into the room, you realize she's right.

But boy, you wish she wasn't.

Go to PAGE 96.

"I'm getting bored up here," the voice complains.

It's headhunter Darius. That's nice.

"Why don't you just give up and open the door?" he suggests. "Then I can start shrinking your head." He laughs.

Oh. Darius wants you to open the door.

That's nice.

You trudge up the stairs to let him in.

It's nice to do what other people tell you. It will always be nice. Right up to

THE END.

You pound the button with your fist. Nothing! "Close, close, close," you mutter.

You hear Jamie make a frightened gurgling sound. You glance up.

Oh, no! Darius is only a few steps away!

You hit the CLOSE DOOR button again and again.

At last, the Transvator doors begin to close. But Darius leaps toward you!

Yes! The doors shut. He crashes against them.

The long blade sticks through the space between the doors. Inches from your throat.

Help!

The knife wiggles. You hear Darius's muffled shouts through the doors. The knife is pulled out with a terrible scrape. Then you hear Darius pounding on the doors.

"Quick!" Jamie shouts. "Push another button before he gets the doors open!"

You stare at the rows of buttons again.

Which one should you choose?

Take a look at PAGE 40.

You push the first button you see. It's marked FAUNA. You wonder what that is.

The floor of the Transvator trembles. The lights flicker, and a groaning sound fills your ears. The Transvator shakes and shudders as if a bulldozer was trying to get in.

"Fasten your seat belts!" Jamie shouts. "This looks like a rough one."

After a few minutes of chaos, the Transvator sets down — *some*where — with a bump. The doors slide open.

You peer out nervously. Are you in a different universe?

The room still looks like Uncle Darius's lab, but it doesn't seem to be as crowded. Then you realize that the inventions are smaller, as if they were designed for little hands.

You and Jamie step into the lab cautiously.

"Just what do you think you're doing?" a voice demands.

You spin around. But there's no one else in the room. No one except a cat. You recognize Sapphire, the cat who ran by you earlier outside. How did she get inside?

She shakes her head. "This room is off-limits to humans. You both know that!" she scolds.

Your mouth drops open in shock.

What's the matter? Cat got your tongue?

Go to PAGE 33.

You and Jamie decide to use the Transvator. You have to save Jamie's real uncle. Who knows what's happening to him in the head-hunting universe?

Besides, you don't want to face *this* Darius alone. Those other universes may be dangerous, but they can't be worse than a knife-wielding maniac.

But first you'll have to make it to the Transvator without losing your head!

Jamie leads you down the hall. You're careful not to make a sound. Uncle Darius's inventions loom all around you. The headhunter could be hiding behind any of them.

Jamie points into the doorway of the lab. The Transvator is just across the room. And the room is empty. No Darius.

You made it!

You and Jamie bolt across the lab. You stab the button of the Transvator with your finger. The machine starts to hum.

Then you hear a rasping sound behind you. Like metal being rubbed against metal.

And footsteps.

You wait nervously for the Transvator doors to open.

They don't.

Turn to PAGE 122.

You examine the Captivator Helmet. It looks like a bicycle helmet, except that wires stick out from it in all directions.

"Does this thing actually work?" you ask doubtfully. "Will it really make someone do whatever I say?"

"I think so," Jamie answers. "Darius hid it down here because he thought people might use it for the wrong reasons."

"Sounds powerful," you comment. "Put it on."

"Me? *You* put it on!" Jamie shoots back.

"No, you!" you insist. To be honest, you're scared to try the helmet.

Jamie sighs. "We're wasting time. One of us has to be the guinea pig."

"I know!" you declare. "We'll play paper, scissors, rock."

"Fine," she agrees. "One, two, three . . . *shoot!*"

What do you choose? Paper, scissors, or rock?

If you choose paper, turn to PAGE 121.

If you choose scissors, cut your way to PAGE 53.

If you choose rock, roll to PAGE 13.

"Ahhhhh!" you scream as you realize what you're holding.

Someone's hand.

But the hand is connected to a body without a head.

Gross!

You drop the hand with a shudder. That's when you notice the entire room is full of headless corpses.

Yikes!

"Wow!" Jamie whispers. "This is where the evil Uncle Darius keeps the rest of the bodies — after he takes the heads."

You gulp. *Your* body might be here. After all, in this universe, your head is a wall ornament!

"Do you think your real uncle Darius is in here?" you ask.

Jamie glances around quickly. "No. He was wearing a Hawaiian shirt. Remember? No one in here has a shirt like that."

"Then he's probably in the basement." You frown. "But it's locked."

"No problem. I think I just found the key," Jamie announces.

She points to a rusty old key lying on the floor. You read the lettering on its label: BASEMENT.

"Oh, boy. I can't wait to go down there," you mutter.

You just wonder what new horrors you'll find.

Head to PAGE 107.

Here's what it says on the side of the van:

ANTI-CHILD PATROL
KIDS CAPTURED 24 HOURS A DAY

"That explains a lot," Jamie mutters.

"That explains *nothing*," you snap.

"Don't you see?" Jamie explains. "Kids are illegal here. That's why there are no children outside playing."

You swallow. "Great. We're illegal here. The police are after us. And we still don't know if this is even the headhunter universe!"

You scan the street. Only a few policemen remain outside on guard. "We'd better make a run for it," you whisper.

"No way! Let's get back to the Transvator," Jamie argues.

"What? Through all those police officers in the house?" you scoff.

Jamie frowns. "Maybe not," she admits. "But we could just stay hidden until they go away."

"That's crazy!" you declare.

"It is not!" Jamie shouts. "*You're* crazy!"

"Hey, who's that in the bushes?" one of the officers yells.

Oops.

Turn to PAGE 30.

ZAP!

With a terrible flash, a huge bolt of lightning shoots from the disk. It strikes the machete in Darius's hand.

You hear a crackling bang — like a gunshot. The force of the electric shock lifts the headhunter into the air.

For a moment you see his skeleton right through his skin!

Then the flash of light fades. You blink away the spots in front of your eyes as the lightning disk slows and stops.

When you can see again, you gasp.

Headhunter Darius! He's burned to a crisp!

"I got him!" you shout down to Jamie and Uncle Darius.

You find some rope and hurl it into the pit. Jamie and her uncle climb out.

Darius pats you on the back. "Great idea!" he booms. "Using the Shock-u-lator to get rid of that maniac. But how did you know which button to push?"

You shrug. "I didn't. The whole thing was a shock to me!"

Go to PAGE 62.

"Let's go back inside, Jamie," you urge.

"Okay," Jamie agrees.

This upside-down universe isn't a place where you'd want to lose your grip.

But as you swing yourself around, you feel the strain in your arms. Your hands weaken.

You catch a glimpse of the sky below you. Your heart starts leaping inside your chest.

"Just a few more rungs!" Jamie cries.

You're almost there. . . .

But will you make it?

Here's a simple way to get your answer. Have you fallen off a jungle gym in the last year?

If you have, go to PAGE 97.

If you haven't, go to PAGE 52.

You grab the sprayer. You've had enough of machetes for one day.

Running back down the hall, you hear Jamie's screams.

"I'm coming!" you cry.

You tear open the back door and charge toward the headhunters. They're lifting Jamie over the fence. She's still struggling to escape from the net.

"Don't move!" you shout.

They stare at you for a moment, then break into laughter.

"Or what?" one asks. "You'll paint us?"

"Don't be stupid," you answer. "This is a . . . a . . . a . . ."

A what?

Maybe you should have picked a weapon you understood better.

"Just put her down!" you order.

Mr. Johnson strides toward you with a wide grin. "Go ahead, spray me," he taunts.

You point the sprayer straight at him. "I will!" you warn him. "I will spray if you don't stop right there!"

But he keeps on coming.

So you squeeze the trigger.

Painted yourself into a corner? Try PAGE 119.

You decide to try FINGERNAILS ON CHALKBOARD. What sound is worse than that?

You pull the trigger.

A horrifying screech comes from the Ear Irradicator. It feels as if someone is scraping a piece of sandpaper right along your nerves!

You bite your tongue, hoping the pain will distract you. The horrible screeching seems to grow louder and louder. You're almost paralyzed with pain. You can barely keep your finger on the trigger.

But you must!

You squint at Darius. He's stopped coming toward you. He stands in the middle of the room, looking stunned.

You squeeze your eyes shut as you force yourself to keep your finger on the trigger.

Finally you can't keep it up any longer. The Ear Irradicator drops from your exhausted hands.

Silence at last! Except for the ringing in your ear.

You open your eyes.

Headhunter Darius stands in front of you.

Uh-oh. Why is he smiling?

Turn to PAGE 135.

You hit the floor. The knife whistles over your head. It misses you by a fraction of an inch.

You roll into Darius's legs. He tumbles over you and onto the floor.

Jumping to your feet, you glance around for Jamie.

She's disappeared!

Darius rises. He leaps toward you, swinging the knife.

"Yaaiiieee!" You stumble backwards, trying to stay out of the reach of the deadly blade. He comes at you again.

Then you realize that you're still holding the shrunken head. *Your* head. You throw it as hard as you can at Uncle Darius.

Direct hit! The tiny head collides with his large one. He falls down again. You turn and run.

You tear down the hall. Where is Jamie?

There hasn't been a sound since you threw the head at Uncle Darius. Maybe he's knocked out! That idea gets your heart rate back to normal.

You come to a room you haven't seen before. Bookshelves line all four walls. Books, magazines, and handwritten notes cover the only table in the room.

Then you hear something behind you.

Uh-oh. You turn around. Slowly.

Gulp. Then turn slowly to PAGE 120.

"Yah!" You scream as you struggle to get away. But headhunter Darius is too strong. You push frantically at the buttons on the control device.

The lights spring on again.

"You moron!" Head-hunting Darius cackles. "It was almost *too* easy. Those buttons glow in the dark."

You stare down at the control device in horror.

He's right, you realize. The buttons are glowing!

Darius could see you the whole time!

He yanks you up by your hair and pulls back the machete for a long, hard swing.

You have the feeling this ending will be a big pain in the neck!

THE END

You gasp in horror. Thousands of insects are flowing out of Mike's sleeve — and into your shirt!

You try to swat the tiny creatures under your clothes, but Mike and the others keep an iron grip on your arms. Your skin crawls with a multitude of little feet.

What's wrong with this universe? Why does everyone talk like a zombie here? And what will these bugs do to you?

If only you could make some sense of it all!

Then you feel pinprick bites from a thousand tiny mouths. You scream and thrash, but you're getting weaker and weaker. . . .

After a while the bites stop hurting so much. In fact, they feel kind of soothing. You feel fine. Just a little sleepy.

The neighbors let you go. You walk slowly toward Uncle Darius's house. Must. Do. Science. Project. You. Think.

You smile. A slow smile.

Bugs. Not. Bad. After. All.

Friends.

Why. Did. They. Ever. Bug. You?

THE. END.

Inside the refrigerator is Uncle Darius. At least, it looks like Uncle Darius.

Except his head is half its normal size! And it's attached to weird, dripping tubes.

"Am I glad to see you!" his little head exclaims.

"What happened to you?" Jamie gasps.

"Isn't it obvious?" the head squeaks. "I got caught by headshrinker Darius. Luckily, he's invented a way to shrink a head without taking it off the body."

"Luckily?" you repeat. You stare at him.

"Sure!" Darius replies. "Better a small head than none at all! Now get me out of here."

You and Jamie help Darius unfold his normal-size body from the cramped refrigerator.

"You were clever, following me in the Transvator," Darius comments.

"We didn't have much choice," Jamie explains. "It was that or get caught by your evil twin."

A tiny frown appears on Uncle Darius's little face. "We'd better get back there and deal with him. He's probably causing all sorts of trouble."

Go to PAGE 41.

You have to disintegrate Darius, you realize. There's no time to make another plan. It's him or you!

You stab the big red button with one finger. "Take that, Darius!" you shout.

The closet door rattles and shakes. Smoke spews into the hall.

What's happening? You squint at the control panel in the darkness.

Hey. Next to the button you pressed is a dial with two settings: DISINTEGRATE and DUPLICATE.

And the dial is set to DUPLICATE.

"Uh-oh," you murmur.

You reach to adjust the dial.

But before you can touch it the closet door springs open!

Turn to PAGE 31. Double-quick!

As you step out of the Transvator, your stomach seems to lurch into your throat. It feels as if you're at the top of a roller coaster, and you're starting to drop.

Only, you're dropping *up!*

"Ouch!" you cry as your head crashes into the ceiling. The rest of your body follows, tumbling into a heap.

You sit up, rub your head, and gaze around the room. It seems normal now that you're on the ceiling.

But Jamie looks pretty funny. She's still in the Transvator, hanging upside down!

"Wow!" she exclaims. "The whole ceiling must be some sort of giant magnet!"

"I don't think so," you reply. "I don't *feel* stuck to the ceiling. I feel normal."

Jamie frowns, then she snaps her fingers. "Hey, I know what's going on. Watch this!"

Take a look on PAGE 125.

You decide to get out of this universe. And fast!

You turn and leap back into the Transvator.

"Come on, Jamie!" you shout.

Sapphire and the black dog stare at you in shock.

Jamie hesitates. "Maybe we should ask them if there are any headhunters here."

"But people don't even *talk* here," you protest. "I doubt if they hunt heads. Besides, I don't want to stay in any universe where I'm not allowed on the furniture!"

"Don't let them get away!" the dog growls. "They might be interesting to study."

"Study?" Jamie repeats. She takes a nervous step back into the elevator.

Sapphire leaps up onto one of the worktables.

"Will you come on, Jamie?" you urge.

Sapphire lifts something in her paws. A dart gun!

"Yikes!" Jamie jumps through the Transvator doors.

You pound the CLOSE DOOR button. The doors *whoosh* shut just as the cat fires the weapon.

Clang! The dart bounces off the metal doors.

Time to get out of here. This universe is for the birds!

Go to PAGE 40.

You rub your jaw. It's sore from clenching so hard. And your unprotected ear is ringing like a car alarm.

"Quick!" Jamie cries as she pulls out her earplugs. "Let's put the Captivator Helmet on him. Then we can make him take us to the real Uncle Darius."

You nod your aching head. Jamie darts down to the basement and returns with the helmet. She kneels and you help her slip it onto the unconscious Darius.

"Wake up," Jamie orders.

Darius lifts his head groggily. He seems confused. His eyes are glassy. But you aim the Ear Irradicator at him, just in case.

"Now do a dance for us," Jamie commands.

Your eyes widen as Darius stands and dances a jig.

"Wow!" you shout. "That helmet thing really works!"

"Great! Now all we have to do is go to the universe of headhunters and free Uncle Darius!" Jamie exclaims.

"Oh, is *that* all?" you mutter.

Turn to PAGE 20.

You hit the button labeled BUGGY.

The elevator shudders and rumbles. You and Jamie brace yourselves. It feels as if you're shooting into the sky!

Finally the shaking stops. The door *whooshes* open.

The lab doesn't seem to have changed at all. You step out slowly, listening. The house is silent.

"Uncle Darius?" Jamie calls.

You search the house, peering nervously into every room.

It seems to be empty.

"Let's look outside," Jamie suggests. "But remember, this could be the head-hunting universe. So be careful!"

You reluctantly open the door. Then you grab Jamie's arm. "Look, it's Mike!" you exclaim.

You watch in surprise as your friend Mike Henderson strolls down the street. He doesn't *look* like a headhunter.

You and Jamie approach him cautiously.

"What's up, Mike?" Jamie asks warily.

When he stops and faces you, a chill runs up your spine.

Take a look at PAGE 65.

Wham! You crash right into Darius.

He staggers and falls into the Disintegrator Closet. You slam the door.

"Got him!" you shout. You raise your fist in victory.

Then a terrible crashing sound comes through the closet door. You and Jamie watch in horror as the wood starts to splinter.

Darius is battering his way out!

"Quick!" Jamie cries. "Push the DISINTEGRATION button!"

"I thought we were just trying to capture him," you object.

"He's getting out!" she yells. "We *have* to disintegrate him."

The idea of disintegrating anyone — even a headhunter — makes you a little queasy.

"Maybe we should run for the basement," you suggest.

What should you do? Run for the basement and search for another invention you can use against Darius?

Or just disintegrate him right now?

Think fast. Darius is seconds from his freedom!

To disintegrate Darius, go to PAGE 89.
To run for the basement, go to PAGE 128.

You and Jamie rush to the window. Your sneakers squelch with water. You wring out your shirt as you stare outside.

You see all of Darius's neighbors emerging from their homes. They form a line in the street, and start a slow procession.

"Zombie parade," Jamie murmurs. "I wonder where they're going."

"Maybe we should join them," you suggest.

"*What?*" She stares at you as if you're totally nuts.

"Just to see what's going on here," you argue. "We need to find a way to fight the bugs, don't we? Anyway, we fooled them before. Just. Talk. Slowly."

Jamie looks worried. "I say we look around for some way to clear the Transvator," she says. "If the Darius in this universe is also an inventor, he may have something we can use."

The idea of poking around the dark house, which might have bugs in every nook and cranny, is pretty creepy. Of course, if you join the zombie parade, who knows where you'll wind up?

What should you do?

To search the house for a way to fight the bugs, turn to PAGE 29.

To join the zombie parade, go to PAGE 69.

The walls of the library are crowded with small glass boxes. Each is lit from below by a tiny burning candle.

And all the boxes hold the same thing. A shrunken head.

The flickering candlelight makes it seem as if the faces are moving. Some look amused, some seem angry.

All of them definitely give you the creeps.

"Look at this," Jamie whispers, pointing at a trophy on the opposite wall.

A cold drop of sweat trickles down your back as you read the inscription.

TO DARIUS JENKINS
FOR MOST HEADS COLLECTED
IN ONE YEAR
LOCAL HEADHUNTERS GUILD

You shudder. This is a terrifying universe!

As you turn away from the trophy, you find yourself facing an empty box on the shelf. You read the little brass label on the glass box.

"No!" you yell. "No!"

Head to PAGE 28 to read the label.

You're almost there. You're going to make it!

But as you reach for the last rung, your slippery fingers slide off the metal.

You're falling!

"Nooo!" you cry. You close your eyes in terror.

Jamie screams your name. The sound fades into silence behind you.

You keep falling. And falling.

After a while you get up the nerve to open your eyes. You gaze up at the ground.

Wow! You can see the countryside spread out above you. It's sort of like being a sky diver.

Except instead of getting closer to the ground, you're getting farther away.

A huge cloud looms below you. It looks so fluffy, almost like a big blanket.

Hey. Maybe it will catch me, you think. In *this* universe, maybe clouds are solid!

Right?

As the cloud grows closer, you get ready for a nice, soft landing.

Land softly on PAGE 113.

Darius grins down at you. "Your head is mine," he calls.

"I'm not afraid of you," you declare, trying to sound brave.

"Then you're dumber than you look!" Darius leaps onto the stairs. He glances suspiciously from side to side.

But he doesn't notice Jamie hanging above him.

"Come on, Darius. Take my head — if you can," you taunt.

Darius licks his lips and steps toward you.

"Now, Jamie!" you shout. She'd better not miss!

Jamie reaches down and drops the helmet onto his head.

"Hey!" Darius tries to pull the helmet off.

"Leave it alone!" Jamie commands.

His hands fall to his sides. An empty expression replaces his evil scowl.

"Now help me down," Jamie orders.

Darius obeys instantly.

Yes! Your plan worked!

Jamie stares straight into his eyes. "Tell me the truth. What did you do with my uncle?"

"I put him in a new invention," he responds.

"*What* new invention?" she asks.

"A machine that shrinks heads," Darius mumbles.

"Oh, no," is all you can say.

Don't shrink from what happens next. Go to PAGE 20.

"Seen. Enough?" Jamie whispers.

"Too. Much," you reply.

You let a few bug-zombies get ahead of you. Then you turn and start to walk away.

"Going. Somewhere?" a man in front of you demands.

You gasp. His face! It's *covered* with bugs.

"Show. Bugs," he demands. You can't even see his mouth move as he speaks. All you can see are swarming bugs.

"Left. Bugs. At. H-h-home?" you stammer.

He doesn't answer. He just leans toward you. He opens his mouth. A stream of bugs pours out from it — and swarms over you!

You feel hundreds of tiny bites all over. At first you try to run, but you quickly lose your will to do anything.

A few minutes later you find yourself walking beside Jamie into the mouth of the giant statue.

Inside, the walls and floors and even the ceiling are covered with the tiny bugs. The sounds of crunching and chomping echo through the halls.

Looks like the bugs are going to eat you. But that's okay.

What's the *bug* deal?

THE END

100

You know this one. "You get younger and younger," you answer.

"Right," the leader declares. "Congratulations! You are now an official Truant!"

The other Truants pat you and Jamie on the back. The leader explains that they spend their days running from hideout to hideout to avoid the police. If they're caught, they're taken to a huge prison known as The School.

"We'd like to join you. But we can't. We need to get back to my uncle's house," Jamie tells them. "We have to save him from a headhunter."

"What's a headhunter?" the leader asks.

"Sort of like an anti-kid patrol," you explain. "But with a supersharp knife."

The Truants shiver, and agree to take you back to Darius's house. You follow them through a series of secret tunnels. You emerge from a manhole just across the street from the house.

You hear sirens in the distance. You and Jamie say a quick good-bye to the Truants.

Then you dash to the house and into the lab. Jamie pushes the Transvator OPEN DOOR button. You scurry inside.

Where will we end up next? you wonder.

End up on PAGE 40.

You whirl around.

Jamie is covered by an enormous net. It must have dropped from a tree — because there's no one around to throw it.

The net is covered with some sort of tiny barbed hooks. They catch in her clothes and hair as she struggles to escape.

"Stay still," you order Jamie. You kneel to untangle her.

Then you hear it. *Thud. Thud. Thud. Thud. Thud.*

You glance up — and gasp. Five people are leaping over the fence and down from the big oak tree. One of them is Mr. Johnson, your science teacher. He looks normal enough.

Except for the long, sharp machete in his hand.

He's a headhunter! They all are!

"Look, we caught Jamie Jenkins," Mr. Johnson exclaims. "She has a good head on her shoulders."

"Not for long!" growls one of the others. They all laugh.

You gulp, one hand covering your neck.

The headhunters seem to be ignoring you. For now. What should you do? Stay and try to free Jamie? Or run for the house and get one of the head-hunting Darius's inventions?

Think fast!

To help Jamie, jump to PAGE 124.

To run to the house for a weapon, head for PAGE 54.

102

"Aagggh!" You shriek and run from the room. You hear Darius's knife slice the air just behind you.

You realize that you're still clutching the box with the shrunken head. You gasp and toss it aside.

What's going on? Jamie said her uncle was a little weird. But cutting your head off is *way* more than weird! That Transvator must have done something to him.

Jamie runs beside you. You spot the front door at the end of the hall.

You hear Uncle Darius charging down the hall after you. His pounding footsteps seem to shake the whole house.

Jamie is faster than you. She reaches the front door and tries to fling it open. But it doesn't even budge!

You crash into her. You both tumble to the floor in a heap.

"Going somewhere?" a voice asks above you.

Your heart seems to stop beating as you stare up at Uncle Darius.

Turn to PAGE 67.

You flail your arms. Your hand grabs the edge of the floor. You hold on for all you're worth.

Yikes! You're dangling over the pit!

You hear Darius and Jamie land below.

Using all your strength, you scramble up onto the floor. You peer down. "Are you all right?" you call.

"I'm okay," Jamie shouts. "But Uncle Darius is knocked out."

The voice of headhunter Darius fills the lab. "You're smarter than you look," he cackles. "But I'll still get your head. Ready or not, here I come!"

"Here, catch!" Jamie cries. Uncle Darius's control device flies up from the pit. You snag it.

"What do I do with this?" you wail.

"How should I know?" Jamie calls back. "Pick a button."

Headhunter Darius appears across the lab, machete in hand. He steps toward you, grinning an evil grin.

You glance desperately at the little device. On it are three glowing buttons. Each has a picture.

Which should you press?

To press the *button, go to PAGE 10.*

To press the *button, go to PAGE 48.*

To press the *button, go to PAGE 56.*

104

"Let's check out this universe," you decide.

Opening the door is a dizzying sensation. The clouds seem to be awfully far below you. It's hard to think of the ground as the sky and the sky as the ground!

You spot a walkway up to the house. It has rungs like a jungle gym leading to a monorail bus stop. You grab the rungs and start toward the bus stop.

Your dizzy feeling grows stronger. Don't look down. Don't look down, you tell yourself.

Or is it, Don't look up?

A funny idea goes through your mind. In this universe you'd never have to rake leaves. They'd just fall into the sky!

But then you think: What happens to the leaves? Do they just keep going all the way to outer space? Where do they end up?

The more you think, the more nervous you get. Your hands start to sweat. And you're getting cramps in your fingers from holding on.

You're only halfway to the bus stop. Maybe you should turn around and go back inside.

Or would it be better to just keep going?

To turn around, turn to PAGE 82.
To keep going, pull yourself to PAGE 118.

No sound is more annoying than a dripping faucet, you think.

You pull the DRIPPING FAUCET trigger. The Ear Irradicator starts making a familiar drip, drip, drip sound.

But it doesn't stop Darius. He's still charging toward you.

Better try something else. Fast!

You squeeze the other triggers.

Nothing happens.

Drip, drip, drip!

You bang the Ear Irradicator on the floor.

It keeps on dripping.

It's just like a *real* leaky faucet. You can't stop it!

You and Jamie turn to run at the exact same time. You crash right into each other!

Headhunter Darius stands over you, grinning. "Two at once!" he exclaims in delight. Then he swings his machete.

Dripping Faucet? What were you thinking?

That was a pretty drippy plan!

THE END

106

You decide to take the Kid Test. After all, you're a kid, right? It should be easy.

The leader of the Truants pulls a tattered book from his pocket.

"Before kids were made illegal, there was a series of books called Goosebumps," he declares. "If you're really a kid, you must have read them."

Of course you have! You nod your head. So far, so good.

"In a book called *The Cuckoo Clock of Doom*, what did the clock do to the hero?" the leader asks. "Did it make him grow old incredibly fast? Or did it take him back in time so he got younger and younger?"

You read that book years ago. Now, what *was* the story?

"Answer carefully," the leader warns. "You only have one chance."

So which was it?

To answer "older and older," go to PAGE 50.

To answer "younger and younger," go to PAGE 100.

You hurry back into the house.

The KEEP OUT sign stares you in the face as you turn the key slowly in the lock.

The door creaks open.

The basement stairs are pitch-black. You can't see a thing!

You start to feel for a light switch. Then you stop, remembering what happened the last time you tried that.

"Maybe we should get a flashlight," you suggest.

"Don't be a wimp. Just find the light switch," Jamie says impatiently.

"You do it!" you snap.

"No way!" She glares at you.

Well? What's it going to be?

To find the switch, feel your way to PAGE 59.
To hunt for a flashlight, go to PAGE 70.

108

The Lance Steel figure begins changing in your hands! It thins out and lengthens, winding around your arms.

"Hey!" you shout. You try to drop it, but you can't. Somehow the body of the toy has transformed — into handcuffs!

"Help, Jamie!" you cry.

But the model train she's holding transforms too. It wraps around her like chains!

"Lance Steel, calling headquarters," the tinny voice says. "We have two children in custody. Request backup."

"No!" you scream. You tug at the handcuffs. Then you bang them hard against the table, trying to break them.

No use. They grip like iron.

A moment later full-size policemen burst into the room. "We've got you now," one of them snarls.

"But we didn't do anything!" Jamie protests.

The police ignore her. They carry you both to a van outside.

"The old toy trick works every time," one of the police officers comments. "Kids can't resist it."

This doesn't make any sense, you think.

Until you see what's written on the side of the van.

Read it on PAGE 32.

You step cautiously into the dark lab. Jamie sticks close to Uncle Darius. You stick even closer to Jamie.

Silence. There's no sign of headhunter Darius.

"Be careful," Uncle Darius cautions. "If I know that Darius, he's got some clever tricks up his sleeve."

You gulp. Maybe the other Darius isn't even here anymore, you think hopefully. Maybe he went out head-hunting.

Then you hear a terrible laugh. "So you've come back!"

Your head whips around, but you don't see anyone. The voice seems to be coming from every direction.

"I've been waiting for you," the voice booms. "I have a special surprise just for you!"

The floor underneath your feet suddenly opens up. A deep black pit yawns below you.

And you're falling fast!

Fall onto PAGE 103.

110

You decide to search for Uncle Darius right away. If this is the headhunters' universe, you don't want to be caught playing with toys!

You explore the house carefully, but find no clues.

"Maybe we should search outside," Jamie suggests.

"Let's just look out the window," you say. "Why risk our necks — or our heads?"

"You have a point," Jamie agrees.

"Weird," she comments, peering through the curtains. "It's Saturday. But nobody's outside playing."

You join her at the window. She's right. You would expect to see some kids playing tag or skateboarding. "Maybe in this universe there's school on Saturdays," you suggest.

Jamie shudders. "Creepy!"

Across the street you spot a neighbor raking leaves.

"That's Ms. Jay," Jamie exclaims. "She's nice." Before you can stop her, she opens the door. "Ms. Jay!" she calls.

The woman seems startled. She drops her rake and runs into her house.

"Now, that's weird too," you comment.

Turn to PAGE 55.

The next day you and Jamie present your project to your science class.

"So how does this thing work?" Mr. Johnson, the teacher, asks.

"Simple. You just put it on your head," you explain.

Mr. Johnson gingerly slips the dented metal helmet onto his bald head.

"And now you explain to the class that we are the smartest kids in school," Jamie says.

"While standing on one foot," you add.

"And flapping your arms like a chicken," Jamie finishes.

"Right," Mr. Johnson mumbles obediently.

You sit back to watch the show.

This is definitely going to be the best science fair ever!

THE END

You hear Jamie's voice, but you're already in the lab.

You feel a burst of excitement. Wait until Darius finds out what you have planned for him!

You're a bit too high up, though. You'll have to bend down to hit his head. Isn't there a height control on these shoes?

You can't find one.

Meanwhile you keep rising. And rising.

A moment later your head bumps the ceiling. "Ow!" you shout.

The shoes keep rising under your feet, shoving your whole body up against the ceiling. Your knees are next to your ears!

"Whoa!" Your shoes hit the ceiling.

You're hanging upside down!

You try to move your feet, but they won't budge. They're pushing against the ceiling, trying to pull you higher.

Darius bursts into the room. He sees you stuck to the ceiling and laughs.

He takes a moment to sharpen his long machete. Why not? He's in no hurry. It's not like you're going anywhere.

Maybe you should have listened to Jamie's warning. Because Darius is swinging the freshly sharpened machete now.

And your neck is right where he wants it.

Which makes this

THE END.

The air must be getting too thin for your brain. Did you think a *cloud* would hold you?

Clouds are just water vapor!

And you *fell* for it.

Plunging through the cloud is just like passing through a chilly fog. When you tumble out the other side, you're soaked.

And the sky is darker. And colder.

Of course. You're getting close to outer space.

Hey! You're about to become an astronaut! That's every kid's dream, isn't it?

Too bad you didn't bring a spaceship. . . .

THE END

A light switch!

"Got it!" you cry. And flick the switch.

ZZZZZAPPPP!

Ever wondered what fifty thousand volts of electricity feels like?

Well, now you know.

"Aaaaagh!" you shriek as the electricity races through your body. You want to let go of the switch. But you can't pry your fingers loose.

Oh, yeah, you think just before your brains fry. The Uncle Darius in *this* universe invents booby traps!

Guess that makes *you* the boob.

THE END

"Run, Jamie!" you shout.

You dart back through the open Transvator doors. Jamie is right behind you.

Then the harpoon gun makes a little noise. *Thwap!*

You spin around. Jamie is holding a hand to her neck. She staggers and falls in the doorway of the Transvator.

"Noooo!" you moan.

You see the cat reloading her gun. You frantically start to drag Jamie into the Transvator. It feels as if she weighs a ton! You reach for the CLOSE DOOR button.

Got it! The doors start to close.

Thwap!

You feel a sharp sting as the mini-harpoon hits your outstretched arm. You reach to push one of the other buttons. Any button! You've got to get out of here!

But your head is swimming.

It's getting dark.

And those buttons are awfully far away. . . .

Go to PAGE 38.

"Uh, we've had enough science for one day," Jamie says quickly.

"Are you sure?" Uncle Darius looks disappointed.

"We're sure," you declare, grabbing Jamie's arm. "But thanks!" You and Jamie dash out of the house.

Outside, Jamie lets out a long sigh. "Phew," she murmurs. "I don't think I could survive another demonstration."

"No kidding," you reply. "But what *will* we do for a science project? Mr. Johnson said if I didn't do well on this project, I might fail!"

"Oh, I have a feeling we'll be getting a good grade." Jamie smiles and holds up a small bag.

"What's in there?" you ask.

"The best science project *ever*," she proclaims, holding the bag toward you.

You snatch it from her hand and tear it open. What can she have grabbed as a souvenir?

When you see what's inside, you can't help but burst out laughing.

Turn to PAGE 35.

The blinding flash startles you. It takes a moment before the spots clear from your eyes.

When you can see again, you stare in horror. The evil Darius lies in a heap at the bottom of the stairs.

"What happened?" you gasp.

"It must have been a booby trap," Jamie answers in a shaken voice. "To catch people trying to sneak in here. But Darius caught himself."

"Boy," you mutter, "that helmet works *too* well. You shouldn't always do what people tell you!"

You creep down the stairs and glance around the room. The only thing there is a machine the size of a refrigerator.

You flinch when you hear a voice coming from it.

"Help me! Help me!"

Jamie opens the door of the machine.

You can't believe what you see.

Turn to PAGE 18.

Keep going, you urge yourself.

Jamie can tell you're losing your cool. "You can make it," she tells you. "Just don't think about it."

Right. She's right.

Just don't think about what happens if you fall.

Don't think about the huge, open sky below you.

Don't think about the coldness of outer space.

You're thinking about it, aren't you?

Well? Aren't you?

A few rungs from the bus stop, you feel your sweaty, cramped fingers start to slip. . . .

Can you make it?

Go to PAGE 97.

The sprayer makes a gurgling noise.

Then a jet of bright red goo spurts onto your head-hunting science teacher. The goo breaks up into long, thin strands. They wrap around him like a thousand fingers.

Mr. Johnson falls to the ground, shrieking. The goo keeps breaking into more and more sticky strands. Soon it covers his entire body.

Then the red gooey mass starts to shrink!

Muffled screams come from within the goo. It's as if your teacher has been covered by a million tiny red boa constrictors!

You stare down at the sprayer in amazement. It must be Darius's newest invention.

When you glance back at your science teacher, the goo has evaporated. Mr. Johnson lies motionless on the ground.

And he's only six inches tall.

He's just like one of the shrunken heads.

Only he's a whole shrunken *person!*

The other headhunters gaze at you with awe.

"Put my friend down!" you order.

Guess what?

They do.

Goo straight to PAGE 11.

You sigh with relief.

Jamie stands in front of you, panting.

"What is with your uncle Darius?" you gasp.

"That's not *my* uncle Darius," Jamie whispers. "Didn't you listen to what he said about other universes?"

You think back — to before your head showed up in a box. "Something about them being the same as this one," you reply. "Except for one deadly difference."

"That's right," she confirms. "But sometimes the same people exist in more than one universe. *That* Uncle Darius came from some other universe." She shudders. "A nasty one."

You clutch your head. Other universes? More than one Uncle Darius? This is all happening way too fast!

"So where is *your* uncle Darius?" you manage to ask.

"He must still be there in the other universe," she explains. Her forehead wrinkles with concern. "He told me about it once. A place where head-hunting is the most popular sport. They even have game shows about it!"

You gulp. Game shows? About *head-hunting?* Then you have a terrible realization.

Hunt for PAGE 71.

You hold your hand out as flat as a pancake. "Paper!" you declare.

You glance down at Jamie's hand. It's curled into a fist. Rock.

Paper covers rock. You win!

"Two out of three!" Jamie protests.

"No way!" you reply. "Put on the helmet."

She frowns, but puts it on. The wires jangle as she fits it over her brown hair. A blank look comes over her face.

You snicker. "You look like a weirdo."

"I look like a weirdo," she answers tonelessly.

Whoa. The helmet really works!

"Tell me how smart I am," you suggest.

"How smart you are," she answers robotically.

"No." You frown. "I mean, tell me I'm super-smart. Even smarter than you!"

"You are supersmart," Jamie drones. "Smarter than me."

Cool! Normally Jamie would punch you in the arm if you tried to pull a fast one like that.

This helmet is excellent!

"All right. You can take it off now," you tell her.

She takes the helmet off. And *then* punches you in the arm.

If your arm isn't too sore, turn to PAGE 64.

"Why won't the Transvator doors open?" you cry.

The footsteps reach the entrance to the lab. You glance back and shudder. Now you can see what that rasping sound was.

Evil Darius is rubbing his knife with a piece of stone.

He's *sharpening* it!

"I've got you now. There's nowhere to hide!" he booms.

The Transvator doors *swish* open. You and Jamie leap inside.

"What are you doing?" Darius throws aside the stone and charges toward you.

You peer frantically around the inside of the Transvator. There are dozens of buttons. But then you spot one that says CLOSE DOOR.

Don't just stand there — push the button on PAGE 75!

The machete hurtles toward you. It whistles through the air like a screaming bird of prey.

You drop to the floor just in time. The knife buries itself into the wall behind you with a *THUNK!*

You gulp at how close it came to slicing your head off.

But there's no time to think about that. Darius is running toward you. He pulls another, smaller knife from his belt.

You raise the Ear Irradicator. There's no time to put your earplug back in. You hope one will be enough.

You aim at the charging headhunter, pointing the weapon right at his head.

Which trigger should you pull?

To pull the DRIPPING FAUCET *trigger, go to* PAGE 105.

To pull the FINGERNAILS ON CHALKBOARD *trigger, go to* PAGE 84.

To pull the DENTIST'S DRILL *trigger, go to* PAGE 23.

You have to try to help Jamie!

You grab the net and yank as hard as you can, ignoring the bite of the barbed hooks. But the barbs stick to Jamie's clothing, and the net stays attached to her.

And catches on your pants legs.

"Get off me!" you shout at the net. You're dragged to the ground as Jamie tries to roll free.

A wave of panic rises in your chest. You kick wildly with your free leg.

Oh, no! Now *both* your legs are tangled in the hooks!

"Well, this one's head should shrink pretty easily." Mr. Johnson laughs. "There's not much in it!"

The headhunters all crack up.

Mr. Johnson grabs you by the hair.

And raises his machete high.

Cut over to PAGE 22.

Jamie does a handstand inside the Transvator. Then she walks forward on her hands. Out of the Transvator.

You watch in amazement as she "falls" up. She lands feetfirst next to you on the ceiling.

"Ta-da!" she cries. "Did you see that?"

You feel dizzy. "Yeah, but what did I see?"

"Simple. Gravity is reversed here," Jamie explains. "Up is down. Down is up. Check it out."

Jamie leads you to a window. You peer out.

Whoa! The cars in the street hang from tracks in the road. A squirrel runs by, clinging to the grass. From where you stand on the ceiling, everything seems to be upside down.

It's actually kind of cool.

"Let's go outside and explore," you suggest.

"Do you think it's safe?" Jamie sounds nervous.

"Sure. Your uncle said that different universes only have *one* difference," you point out. You're proud of yourself for remembering. "So they can't have headhunters here."

"I hope you're right," Jamie murmurs.

You feel a sudden pang of doubt. Should you go outside?

Or should you just get back in the Transvator?

To go outside, turn to PAGE 104.
To return to the Transvator, turn to PAGE 40.

You decide to search for a key to the basement. In a universe full of headhunters, that seems a lot safer than going outside!

You and Jamie check the kitchen first. Then the lab, the closets, everywhere. You even search all the shelves in the library. You feel as if the little heads on display are watching you. It's a totally creepy feeling.

You don't find a key anywhere.

You kick a wall in frustration. "What do we do now?"

Jamie bites her lip. "If we can't open the basement door, maybe we can go *through* it," she says.

"Huh?" You stare at her.

"Come on." Jamie leads you down the hall to a big closet. "When I was searching for the key, I found this."

She flings open the closet door.

"What in the world is *that?*" you exclaim.

Find out on PAGE 66.

"I am a big doofus," you recite. Why not?

Jamie is laughing her head off. "This is great!"
She's having fun. That's nice.

"So, doofus," she commands, "do a handstand!"

You vaguely remember that you're not very good at handstands. But if Jamie wants you to do one, you'll try.

Your hands hit the dusty floor and your feet shoot into the air. Jamie laughs.

This is nice.

But then you start to lose your balance. You crash into a shelf full of mechanical parts. The shelf tips and the parts start to rain down.

One hits Jamie in the head. She cries out and falls to the floor.

You stand up, wondering what to do next.

Jamie isn't moving. She isn't telling you what to do.

That *isn't* nice. You need someone to tell you what to do.

A few minutes later you hear a voice from behind the door at the top of the stairs.

Maybe the new voice will tell you what to do.

Get your orders on PAGE 74.

You decide to run for the basement.

"Come on!" you yell, bolting down the hall.

You hear Jamie's footsteps pounding behind you. Then you hear a sickening crash as the door of the Disintegrator Closet bursts open.

"That way!" Jamie cries, pointing toward the lab.

You spot the basement door ahead.

But you can also hear Darius charging after you.

You reach the door and yank it open. Jamie leaps through. You follow. She throws the bolt — just as Darius crashes against the door.

He pounds furiously on it. Will it hold?

It seems to be holding. Whew! At least this door is stronger than the one on the Disintegrator Closet.

"We're stuck here," Jamie mutters. "There's no way out except this door."

You gulp.

Outside there's silence. Darius seems to have given up on breaking down the door. For now.

You glance at Jamie. "What exactly are we hoping to find in the basement?"

Find out on PAGE 25.

The Truants scatter, darting through secret doors. You and Jamie try to follow, but the doors slam in your face.

"Gotcha!" A big policeman grabs you by your shirt.

An even bigger officer holds a struggling Jamie. "You two are going to The School!" He bellows with laughter.

Some school. It's a huge gray prison where kids are kept until they're eighteen years old. You figure it will be too late to rescue Uncle Darius by then.

Of course, you and Jamie probably won't be around that long. Not when every kid in The School can tell what you are just by looking at your face.

They whisper through your cell door at night, "We're going to get you, traitor."

And sooner or later they will. . . .

THE END

Before you can answer, the Truants pounce on you and Jamie. They drag you through a trapdoor into a tunnel. You hear the police crashing into the warehouse above.

The Truants lock you and Jamie in a dark room.

You bang on the door. "We aren't spies! We didn't mean to lead them to you!" you shout. "Honest!"

A window in the door slides open. The leader peers in.

"Now you'll discover what we do to traitors," he threatens. "Look behind you."

You glance behind you. The room is full of toys. That's not so bad. Is it?

Then you remember. In this universe, toys *hate* kids. They're all programmed to trap you — or worse!

One by one the toys roll, crawl, and scuttle toward you. Toy fire engines, action figures, airplanes, even happy-faced little dolls.

You never knew playtime could be so serious. Well, in this universe it is.

Dead serious!

THE END

You decide to check out a few of the toys.

You spot a Lance Steel action figure. He's the coolest. He can do kung fu kicks and punches. Plus he comes with wrist missiles, and a helmet with a laser beam.

Any universe with Lance Steel in it can't be all bad. . . .

You lift the figure carefully off the worktable. It's over a foot tall — much bigger than the Lance figures in your own universe.

As you turn the figure around in your hands, a little static pop like a police radio comes from it.

"This is Lance Steel," a tinny voice announces.

"Hey, cool! It talks!" you exclaim, "I wish we lived in *this* universe."

"You are under arrest," the little voice continues, "for the crime of being a child!"

What a weird thing for an action figure to say, you think.

Then something even weirder happens.

Turn to PAGE 108.

132

You choose rock again.

You thrust out your fist, hoping Jamie will choose scissors.

But she sticks with rock too.

It's a tie again!

"All right. Let's do it until we get a winner!" you command.

What should you do? Will Jamie stay with rock or not?

If you choose rock again, turn to PAGE 13.
If you choose paper, turn to PAGE 121.
If you choose scissors, turn to PAGE 53.

"Take it off," you command.

Darius reaches up —

And takes off the helmet!

Oops. You should have been more specific.

The moment the helmet leaves his head, Darius's blank expression disappears. The familiar evil smile returns.

Jamie reacts first, dashing toward the lab. You turn to follow, but Darius's hand locks around your neck with an iron grip.

"Going somewhere?" he growls in your ear.

You hear the Transvator's doors close as Jamie jumps inside.

Maybe she'll try to rescue you.

Maybe not.

Then you feel the helmet fitting down over your head.

And suddenly your mind is a perfect blank.

Darius opens the basement door and orders, "Go downstairs."

You obey, of course. What else can you do?

It's nice to obey. You feel very calm.

Then you see what's in the basement.

Turn to PAGE 49.

You blink your eyes in disbelief. But when they open again, nothing has changed.

It still looks like Uncle Darius's house, except for one thing.

The furniture is all on the ceiling.

Okay. This is definitely another universe.

Wow!

"What's the deal?" you whisper. "Crazy interior decorators?"

"Maybe it's just to confuse us," Jamie guesses. "So the headhunters can cut off our heads while we're busy looking up."

You gulp. That seems like a lot of trouble just for a couple of heads.

"Uncle Darius," Jamie calls nervously.

No answer.

"Maybe we should take a look around," you suggest.

You step cautiously out of the Transvator.

Then something *really* strange happens.

Flip to PAGE 90.

He grins broadly. "Thank you! That's one of my two favorite noises," he declares.

You stare in disbelief. Is he serious?

"Wh-what's your other favorite noise?" you stutter at last.

"The sound of neckbones cracking when I twist them!" Darius laughs heartily. "But words can't describe it. Here, let me demonstrate."

And he grabs your neck in his powerful hands.

You're too exhausted to struggle much. Darius starts to twist. "Listen!" he commands.

It sounds to you like this is . . .

THE END.

136

"Let me run just one more test, and maybe I'll bring you back a souvenir!" Darius bounds toward the machine.

He pushes the button, and the doors slide open. He jumps inside, and the doors close.

"He *is* excitable," you comment to Jamie.

"In the extreme," she mutters.

The Transvator starts to groan and shudder. Whoa! The whole house starts to shake, making your teeth rattle. The lights dim.

Finally the machine trembles to a stop. When the doors slide open, Darius glances around. He seems confused, as if he can't figure out where he is. His eyes land on you and he smiles.

"I have something for you," he growls. His voice sounds weird. Different, somehow. He hands you a box.

You open it. And scream.

Inside the box . . . there's a shrunken head!

And one more thing. It's *your* head.

Get ahead on PAGE 5.

About R.L. Stine

R.L. Stine is the most popular author in America. He is the creator of the *Goosebumps, Give Yourself Goosebumps, Fear Street,* and *Ghosts of Fear Street* series, among other popular books. He has written more than 250 scary novels for kids. Bob lives in New York City with his wife, Jane, teenage son, Matt, and dog, Nadine.

GIVE YOURSELF Goosebumps®

...WITH 20 DIFFERENT SCARY ENDINGS IN EACH BOOK!

R.L. STINE

$3.99 EACH

- -

Scare me, thrill me, mail me GOOSEBUMPS now!

Available wherever you buy books, or use this order form.

Scholastic Inc., P.O. Box 7502, Jefferson City, MO 65102

Please send me the books I have checked above. I am enclosing $_____ (please add $2.00 to cover shipping and handling).
Send check or money order—no cash or C.O.D.s please.

Name _____ Age _____

Address_____

City _____ State/Zip_____

Please allow four to six weeks for delivery. Offer good in the U.S. only. Sorry, mail orders are not available to residents of Canada.
Prices subject to change.

© 1998 Parachute Press, Inc. GOOSEBUMPS is a registered trademark
of Parachute Press, Inc. All rights reserved.

GYG798

SCHOLASTIC

 PARACHUTE

Log on for Scares!

EAU CLAIRE DISTRICT LIBRARY

Scholastic presents

G™

Goosebumps
ON THE WEB!

http://www.scholastic.com/Goosebum

- The latest books!
- Start your own Goosebumps reading club!
- Author R.L. Stine's tips on writing!
- Really gross recipes!
- Craft ideas!
- Exclusive contests!
- How to get Goosebumps stuff: sportswear, CD-ROMs, video releases and more!
- Interactive word games and activities!

© 1997 Parachute Press, Inc. GOOSEBUMPS is a registered trademark of Parachute Press, Inc. All rights reserved.   GWEB12